CHEERY CHARMS

Winter Witches of Holiday Haven Book 6

❧❧❧

BELLA FALLS

Evermore Press

Contents

RECIPES

Winter Witches Books by Bella Falls

Sleigh Spells

Cheery Charms

Merry Mischief

Enjoy the whole Winter Witches of Holiday Haven Series!

Hark! The Herald

Editor Archer Olsen   Holiday Haven's Local Paper   July 2021

The Winter Witches are Back!

Despite the summer heat, the Winter Witches are cooler than ever! Join Rory, Lumi, Star, Carolyn, and Rudie and celebrate Christmas in July--Holiday Haven style!

We've got five new cozy mysteries coming your way soon, and they're brimming with magic, humor and holiday cheer!

Introduction

It's time to *shell*-ebrate! Tis the sea-*sun* for a little solstice fun in Holiday Haven!

Aurora Hart's life has never been better. She's got a successful business as an ice sculpture artist, a group of loyal friends in the Humbugs, and a hot bear of a boyfriend. Her reputation as the savior of Christmas gets her more attention than she wants, especially when the event planner for the summer solstice celebration wants her help making something special.

Everything's going swimmingly until something goes terribly wrong. Now, all of the attention is focused on Rory, except for all the wrong reasons. Accused of being the reason things for the festivities are ruined, she needs the help of her fellow Humbugs to find who's really behind it all. They need to work fast if they're to keep all hope for Holiday Haven from melting away.

Water you waiting for? Get cozy and read *Cheery Charms*, the second book by Bella Falls in the Winter Witches of Holiday Haven series. And be sure to check out the other magical mysteries of the **Winter Witches of Holiday Haven series**!

Chapter One

Magic flowed down my arms and out of my hands, shaping the block of ice in front of me. With my ice sculpture business so successful in just a few months, I no longer doubted my powers or abilities. Most of the time, I took great pleasure in my work. However, the piece I was working on in this moment made me a tad uncomfortable.

"Be sure to get my good side," Cora called out as she held her pose with great care. "And don't go trying to make me slimmer or shaving off some of my curves. I want my darling Walter to appreciate me as a bathing beauty just as I am."

I giggled at my friend's audacious courage and bit my tongue to keep from making any remarks about her current outfit. "Yes, ma'am." My fingers sculpted the ruffles on the hem of her swimming skirt with great care.

She shot me a sideways glance as she harrumphed. "You know I can read your mind, missy. When you get to be my age, you figure out pretty quick that it's better to accept and appreciate the rewards of your life's journey rather than resent them."

"Sounds like good advice," I agreed.

"And don't you dare go judging my choice of outfit," she jumped in before I barely finished. "You're lucky I didn't go with my first choice to have you sculpt me in my favorite suit."

I finished melting in some of the polka dots from her outfit into the ice. "Which suit is that?"

"My birthday one." With a gleeful cackle, Cora wiggled her eyebrows at me.

I swallowed hard and did my best not to show any reaction. Unfortunately, I couldn't scrub away the image that appeared in my mind and refused to go away. With extra determination, I willed my magic to hurry up and finish my friend's sculpture of the month. For once, I wished I could pay her actual money in exchange for her services as my business assistant.

Jingle bells tinkled as someone opened the front door of Pine & Dandy. "What in tarnation is going on in my store?" Amos called out as he walked back in our direction.

Cora jumped in surprise and grabbed her robe, barely getting it around her body before the shop owner joined us. "What are you doing here?"

Amos stood next to us, his hands planted firmly on his hips. "I think that question is better asked of the two of you."

My sassy assistant finished tying the sash of her robe before strutting up to stand in front of him. "I was cashing in on my monthly payment if you must be so nosy. Since it's almost time for the summer solstice celebration, I thought I'd give my loving husband something to look forward to."

Amos's eyes turned to me, and my cheeks heated under his scrutiny. Keeping my focus on the final details of Cora's bathing beauty sculpture, I kept myself out of the conversation and gave my absolute best to portray every lump, bump, and imperfection of my friend per her request. Once finished, I stood back from the ice and checked it over until I gave it my final approval. Amos and Cora both stood nearby and looked it over.

Cora narrowed her eyes at the shop owner. "Watch what you say about my figure, Amos Pine, or so help me, I will hex you so hard you won't wake up until it's Christmas time again."

My cantankerous fellow Humbug held up his hands in surrender. "I was only going to compliment Rory's ability to capture such a lifelike rendering.

Your skills have really improved in such a short time."

"And that's all you have to say?" Cora challenged.

Amos blinked at her in mock innocence. "I think it's great." He clamped his lips tight, refusing to add anything else.

After a tense moment, Cora gave up and gathered the rest of her clothes in her arms. "I'm going to go change and then head home. I'll make the arrangements to have this delivered to my house tomorrow so it can be a proper surprise." She sashayed over to me and gave me a quick motherly peck on the cheek. "And he's not wrong, you know. You really have become quite the talented artist. Like I've been saying all along."

My cheeks heated hotter than my own fire abilities, and I grabbed the faded sheet I had stashed next to me to cover the sculpture until my faithful assistant collected her bounty tomorrow.

Amos stayed close to me until he wrinkled his nose and pointed at the ceiling. "What in the world are you listening to?"

A new instrumental Hawaiian melody played through the store speakers. "Cora thought it would help set the mood."

I waited for my grumpy friend to make a bitter complaint, but he listened to it for a moment before shrugging his shoulders. "Well, at least it's a change from holiday music played on unending repeat. Of course, that will start all over again after the celebration." He grumbled something unintelligible under his breath.

Taking a risk, I threw an arm around his shoulder and drew him in for a side hug. "Aw, come on. I thought everybody was looking forward to the solstice thing."

Amos stiffened under my touch. "Have we met?" he grouched.

I let him go with a sigh. "Well, I thought maybe you were someone different since you handled seeing Cora's masterpiece with such aplomb.

With a snort, he gestured for me to head to the back exit of the store that led to the entrance of the Break Room. "You seem to have forgotten that I used to be a loving husband once." A sad silent pause followed his statement, but he cleared his throat and continued. "I know how to keep my nose out of trouble, especially with women like Cora."

As we made our way down the intentionally darkened hallway towards the bar where my bear shifter of a boyfriend waited for me, I couldn't help but wonder if Amos's heart would ever heal. Although the old guy would never admit to it, he had changed just as much as I had in a short amount of time. Maybe letting others into our lives and allowing ourselves to feel and experience more would be good for both of us as time marched on.

"There's my girl!" Wyatt exclaimed from behind the wooden bar as Amos and I appeared in the doorway.

Despite knowing he must be in his usual place behind the bar, I could barely spot my big, tall man behind all the crates piled high with colorful fruits.

"I might be here, but where are you?" I teased. "Amos, have we entered the notorious Break Room or a tropical food market?"

"I have no idea, but I better be able to have my usual," he grunted in pure annoyance.

Wyatt waved me over, his face beaming over the tops of pineapple fronds. It took a little bit of effort on my part not to run to him like a giddy girl, instead throwing a little extra sway into my sashay. The handsome bartender wiped his hands with a towel and made his way around the bar to greet me.

He captured me in his arms, gazing down at me with warm eyes. "How was your day, dear?"

"Much better, now that I get to spend time with you." Even as the words left my mouth, I tasted the truth of them.

Amos gagged behind me. "I need at least two beers to help me wash away all that sickeningly sweet crap. And put it on *your* tab." With crotchety resignation, he sauntered off to join Rocky at the end of the bar.

Wyatt's chest vibrated against me as he let out a rumbling chuckle. "I'll get Nutty right on that." He kissed the top of my head and then the tip of my nose before planting his lips on mine.

The predictable cacophony of whistles and cat calls followed, and we broke away from each other all too soon.

"I'm so glad you're here," he admitted, flashing me the same bright smile that dazzled me every time. "How did Cora's monthly payment turn out?"

Instead of the finished ice sculpture, the mental image of my assistant's body without a stitch of clothing on flashed in front of my eyes, throwing proverbial cold water on my heated mood. There weren't enough drinks in the entire place to erase it, but I could sure as well try.

"It was fine, but I could definitely use some refreshments."

Wyatt raised an eyebrow, perhaps suspecting that I was keeping something from him. But instead of questioning me further, he made his way back to his usual position and fetched my custom beer stein made of ice that I had created for each of us Humbugs. "Then you've come to the right place." He poured some ice water instead of alcohol into the mug. "But I'll bet you could use a little of this to replenish after a long day's work with your magic."

In most of my life, I'd never had anyone in the world take care of me. It had taken a lot of effort on my part in the first few months of my new relationship to accept that someone else cared for me, and that it was okay to accept help and kindness from others. Wyatt had been patient since the beginning of *us*, giving me space to grow and discover who I was and wanted to be in this new existence in Holiday Haven.

I took several gulps, almost finishing half of the water. While Wyatt poured me some more, I gestured at the fruit covering most of the bar except the small corner at the end where Rocky, Amos, and Nutty sat chatting.

"So, I'm assuming there's a good explanation for all of this?" I snagged a bright red strawberry from a nearby crate and bit into it, emitting an obscene groan of delight at its ripe sweetness.

Wyatt eyed me with a look that usually preceded one of our make out sessions and cleared his throat. "There is, but if you're going to make noises like that, I'll let you eat all of it."

"Challenge accepted," I said, grabbing a slice of watermelon and bit into it. "Oh sweet Santa, it's been so long since I've eaten fruit this ripe." Sticky juice dribbled down my chin.

He handed me a napkin. "I've been tasked with creating some drinks for our solstice celebration, and since it's a summer event, I decided to try some new things. It's been kind of fun to use my bartending skills again. I'm out of practice since my typical customer doesn't ask for anything that requires a lot of effort or imagination."

"Hey, I resemble that remark," Amos barked from his end of the bar.

I chuckled and got comfortable on my stool. "Well, what have you come up with so far?"

Wyatt flashed an enthusiastic grin. "Glad you asked. Let me make you something and see what you think."

I watched with fascination as he leaped into action. He dragged the blender closer to him and got busy adding ingredients to it. Fresh fruit was chopped with such skill that the blade of the knife became a blur. After one measured pour from a bottle, he noticed me watching with great intent. A cocky smile spread on his lips, and he tossed the bottle in the air. It flipped a couple of times, and I gasped in fear of it crashing to the floor. When he caught it and placed it back on the shelf with a wink, I laughed at his cockiness.

"Stop showing off for your woman and just make her the danged drink, why don't you," Amos yelled from his bar stool at the end.

"Aw, I like watching him," Rocky countered. "He's acting like all the heroes in the romance books I read."

Nutty scampered down the length of the bar and scrambled over a crate of coconuts. "Yeah, yeah, I wanna see if he'll drop one of the bottles."

I grabbed one of the coconuts that had fallen to the floor and placed it in front of my squirrel roommate. "Here, this particular nut is almost as big as you."

His tail twitched as he held onto it, leaned his head against the dark brown husk, and rapped his knuckles on its hairy surface. "I don't think it's ripe."

Wyatt nodded at his furry help. "I'll be cutting those open and hollowing some out for drinks later. And now for the secret ingredient." He pulled out a large metal container and sat it by his feet.

Gripping the edge of the bar, I balanced myself and leaned forward to see. "What is it? Ice?" I didn't get what was so special about that.

He scooped some of the bright white frozen substance and added it to the blender. "I'm saving the reveal until after you taste it." With a click of the switch, the bar machine whirred to life with a deafening roar.

Wyatt grabbed a hurricane glass from behind him and wiped it with a towel. Turning it upside down, he dipped the edge of the glass in a shallow container of liquid and then covered the wet area with some sort of sparkling granules, setting it to the side. With a smaller knife, he picked one of the strawberries and made careful slices with surgical precision while holding it in his fingers. When he was ready, he turned off the blender and poured the pinkish red drink into the glass. Taking the cut strawberry, he fanned it out and placed it with great care on top.

"I hope this tastes good," he said with weighted anticipation, placing his masterpiece in front of me. "I'd offer you a straw, but I want you to get the full experience."

I'd never been much into fancy drinks, but I raised the glass in the air to toast the skills of its maker. The rim of the glass tasted salty, spicy, and sour all at the same time, but the second the frosted drink hit my tongue, I couldn't get over the explosion of tastes going on in my mouth.

I licked my lips as I finished my first sip. "That is completely amazing! What is it?"

"You really like it?" Wyatt stared at me with earnest hesitation.

To reassure him, I savored another sip, still marveling over the taste combinations dancing in my mouth. "I was expecting something overly sweet, but there's so much more to it. Whatever you have on the rim, it's salty and sour but it's almost got a kick to it as well."

He wiped his hands on the towel, but his eyes twinkled with pride at my approval. "That's crystallized sugar with tajin, which has salt, lime, and red chilies in it. Plus, the spice combo is red, which goes with the whole aesthetics of the drink."

Nutty wanted to taste my drink, and I debated whether I could bring myself to share any with him. Seeing my inner struggle, Wyatt took a shot glass and created a mini version for my roommate, placing it in front of him.

The squirrel sniffed at the contents a few times, his tail twitching with each whiff. He stuck his tongue out and tasted the spiced sugar on the rim with tentative expectation. Once satisfied, he lifted the shot glass in both hands and tipped it back to taste the mixed goodness.

Nutty smacked his lips a few times and cocked his head to the side. "Tastes sweet and spicy, which doesn't make sense because it's making the insides of my head feel like it's been left outside on Christmas Day."

"That's called brain freeze. But Nutty's right. It's got the perfect balance of sweet and spicy with a kick of heat, which really is interesting because it's frozen," I agreed.

My roommate pointed at me. "Yeah, yeah, what she said."

"But is it too spicy? Or not enough? Should there

be more sweetness to it? Or maybe a splash more of lime juice?" Wyatt grilled us, crossing his arms over his broad chest with professional concern.

Wanting to give him my best answer, I took one more sip. As I let the contents consume my mouth, I contemplated the options the expert bartender had given us. "Maybe a little more lime, but really, I think it's practically perfect as is."

Wyatt threw the towel over his shoulder and grinned at me. "I can try that with the next batch."

Curiosity got the best of Rocky and Amos, and they had inched their way down the bar until they sat next to the rest of us. Wyatt prepared them each smaller glasses of the same drink and beamed with pride when they added their compliments.

"So, what's in this girly monstrosity?" Amos snarked.

"I don't think it's a girly drink since I like it. And I'm definitely not a girl," Rocky defended. "That would make it a rock troll-y drink."

Amos rolled his eyes. "Fine." He straightened up and adopted a weirdly serious look on his face. "Pardon me, my good barkeep. But pray tell, what ingredients have you added to your fine creation that can be imbibed by any fine patron?"

Wyatt snickered as he disassembled the blender to clean it out. "It's pretty much a strawberry margarita for the base of it with two types of tequila, fresh strawberries, lime juice," he winked at me, "and some simple syrup I infused with jalapeños to give it an extra kick."

"That's the spiciness that's tickling the back of my throat," Rocky stated, holding up his glass to inspect it.

"But what's the secret ingredient?" I pushed, leaning over the bar to look at the metal container.

Wyatt glanced down at it with mischievous glee. "I obtained that in payment for a favor. Let's just say I know somebody who provided me with some very special snow in exchange for something only I can give them."

Nutty finished the rest of his drink and slammed the shot glass on the bar. "It's snow infused with Santa's magic."

My eyebrows shot up into my hairline. "That's from Santa?"

"Way to keep a secret there, Nut," Wyatt groaned. "How did you know?"

Our squirrel buddy glanced between the bar owner and the rest of us. "What? Santa always trades you something for your moonshine. Everybody knows that."

Amos snorted. "That's actually kind of true."

"Yeah, but we're not supposed to, you know, actually talk about it," Wyatt said. "What will Mrs. Claus think?"

"Clara?" I asked. "Oh, she already knows. If she didn't want her beloved husband to have access to your secret stash, do you honestly believe she wouldn't have shut it down long ago?"

I thought about the woman who'd become my idol and mentor in such a short period of time. Although we didn't hang out all the time together, I knew she would answer my call if I ever needed something, and that helped my roots grow deeper in my new hometown.

Wyatt waved his towel like a flag of surrender. "You're right. The snow probably comes from her magic anyway. It's never ending no matter how much I use, and it always stays cold and perfectly slushy."

Amos finished his drink with a large gulp and sighed audibly. "So, what did you name this baby?"

"Well, if it meets approval, I'll call it a Fire and Ice. In honor of your powers." He tipped his head at me.

My heart pounded faster inside my chest. "You're naming the drink after me?"

Wyatt tried to shrug it off in front of the rest of our friends, but his intense gaze warmed me from head to toe. "Of course. That's why I want it to be perfect because that's what I think you and your magic are."

My mouth opened and closed but I couldn't find

words to express the whirling emotions welling up inside of me.

"But between you and me, I'll be calling the drink The Rory," he added with a wink. "Whatever its name ends up being, I think it'll be the best drink at the solstice celebration."

"That's good to hear," a stranger's voice rang out through the room, her accent very similar to Wyatt's.

A woman dressed in a smart navy-blue suit and some ridiculously high heels stood in the doorway to the place. Her dark stained lips spread into a cordial smile filled with too much enthusiasm and fake friendliness.

She pranced inside the place and strutted toward our group, her eyes trained directly on Wyatt. When she reached the bar, she positioned herself right next to me but barely acknowledged my existence. "Because that's what I expect for any event that I put together. The absolute best!"

Chapter Two

"I see you got my delivery," the woman declared, gesturing at all the fruit.

Wyatt dropped his defensive scowl. "This is all your doing? Then you must be—"

"Pandora Ashmore," the lady finished, extending a perfectly manicured hand out. "I'm the head witch and event planner who's in charge of Holiday Haven's solstice celebration. And you must be Wyatt Berenger, best bartender in the region. It's such a pleasure to meet you in person, and I'm glad to put a face to the name." She captured Wyatt's hand in a delicate greeting.

It took me all of two seconds to check this girl out. Not much older than me but definitely more put together. Every dark hair on her head was swept into a perfect updo. Her tailored outfit hugged every inch of her curves. The makeup she wore accentuated her natural beauty. And I marveled at her ability to wear high heels and not fall flat on her round behind while traipsing around any part of the North Pole.

My boyfriend tilted his head to the side, his eyes narrowing with interest. "Your accent. You sound like you're from the South like me."

Pandora tittered with amusement. "Why, yes, I am. Born and raised in Georgia, which I guess makes me a Southern peach."

Wyatt pointed at his chest. "My people are from the Smokey Mountains of North Carolina."

"Oh, I loved visiting there as a kid," she exclaimed, still gripping my boyfriend's hand. "Such beautiful scenery, especially in the fall with all the colors of the leaves."

"My grandpappy's business used to get slammed at that time of year. He paid me double to help him out while all the tourists were there." My boyfriend beamed as he talked about his former home. "I haven't been back in...well, it's been a while."

Pandora finally let go of his hand as she continued to gush. "I make it back to visit my family about once a year, but I couldn't turn down the amazing opportunities I have here in the North Pole."

"This is a magical place to be," I interjected, forcing myself into the conversation.

The lady clutched the pearls around her neck.

"Oh my heavens, where are my manners. I just got all caught up in feeling like it was some kind of homecoming with Mr. Berenger here. Bad Pandy," she scolded herself. "And you are?"

"Aurora Hart," I answered, the tone of my voice a little sharper than I had intended.

Pandora squealed and rushed forward, encasing me in a tight hug. "Oh my lands, I didn't know I would find you here as well. Fate is definitely smiling down on me today."

While still wrapped in her arms, I glanced at Wyatt with surprise. His amused chuckle did nothing to help me.

She let me go and took a step back, the smile on her dark-stained lips still wide. "It is such a pleasure meeting *the* Aurora Hart. The one who saved Christmas by creating the big man's new sleigh and winner of the Seasonal Spirit Awards."

I straightened my disheveled sweater, becoming very aware of the shlubby appearance of my own clothes. "I didn't win the SSA's. Our whole town did."

Pandora waved me off with her manicured fingers. "Oh, but if it weren't for your heroic contribution, I'm not so sure if the prize would have gone to Holiday Haven. From what I understood, Garland Gale was all but a shoe in for the win. But if you hadn't won, then I wouldn't be here setting up the entire event. See what I mean by fate? This was all just meant to be."

The more she bubbled with enthusiasm, the stronger her accent became. While I found Wyatt's absolutely endearing and a little sexy, hers grated on my nerves a bit.

"Hey, Panda, if we introduce ourselves, will we all get hugs, too? Or are those saved for *the* Aurora Hart?" Amos asked, shooting me a sarcastic glance.

Nutty waved his hand in the air. "Yeah, yeah, maybe I should wear a T-shirt that says I'm *the* Aurora Hart's roommate."

A brief shadow of displeasure clouded Pandora's eyes, but her smile never wavered. "Of course."

In quick succession, I introduced the rest of the Humbugs sitting at the bar. "And you've already met my boyfriend, Wyatt," I highlighted, giving him a purposeful wink.

"You two are together?" Her voice raised another octave in delight. "Bless your heart, that makes things even more interesting. I think I might have one of my brilliant ideas coming." She tapped the corner of her mouth with her polished nail. Now, where has my assistant gone? Mistletoe!"

Out of the corner of my eye, I spotted something struggling to float in the air. As the figure got closer to us, I realized why the figure was bobbing up and down. Pale pink gossamer wings flitted with great effort as the smaller fairy attempted to approach while burdened with a large leather handbag in her clutches. With every wing flap, a little bit of sparkling pale pink dust sprinkled underneath her.

I rushed over to help ease her burden. "Here, I can carry that for you."

The fairy stopped midair and stared at me in surprise. She blew a strand of her green hair away from her face and attempted a smile. "That's so nice of you."

Pandora beat me to it, retrieving the heavy bag herself. "Don't mind Mistletoe. She's much stronger than she looks. Now, let me look at my schedule and see if I have any availability." She pulled out a leather portfolio and opened it up.

I checked with Wyatt to see if he understood what she was doing. He shrugged at me as he wiped down the bar in front of him. As Pandora muttered to herself while flipping through the pages of her calendar, I stood in front of her in awkward silence.

"The whole summer solstice festivities should be a lot of fun," I admitted, breaking the tension with small talk. "I'm interested to see how they're going to bring a summer atmosphere to the biggest winter wonderland in the world."

"Oh, Miss Ashmore has been working hard on making it something special," the fairy interjected. "I'm absolutely amazed she's been able to pull off—"

"That's enough, Mistletoe," Pandora snapped for the first time. Noticing that all eyes flashed toward her, she broke the tension with a lilting titter. "I mean, I want it to be a surprise when Miss Hart visits the site. And why don't you accompany her, Mr. Berenger? Perhaps you can give us a sample of the drinks you're creating with this bounty I sent you so we can choose the best ones."

"Call me Wyatt," my boyfriend insisted, much too quickly for my liking. "I'll be happy to accommodate you as long as it works for Rory as well."

The fairy assistant's wings quivered a little and more pink dust floated to the ground. "Oh wow, Rory Hart? Like, the one who made Santa's new sleigh? I read every single thing written about you and watched the coverage of it over and over again on the Winternet."

Nutty darted off his spot on the bar and scurried over to me, climbing up my body and positioning himself on my shoulder. "Rory is awesome," he agreed, holding onto my ear while leaning forward to talk to the fairy. "She makes the best roommate. Keeps the space nice and clean and doesn't eat any of my personal stash of nuts."

Mistletoe giggled at my furry roommate's enthusiasm. "I'm very pleased to meet her in person."

"Enough chit-chat." Pandora snapped her fingers to get her assistant's attention before tapping the calendar with her finger. "Here, why don't the two of you come by at ten in the morning the day after tomorrow. That would give me time to let you see the whole venue in all its glory. Aurora, you and I can talk about your contributions to the celebration, and Wyatt, maybe you can assist in setting the bar up properly while you create your amazing concoctions for me."

With a nod of his head, Wyatt deferred the decision to me. While I knew I didn't have anything on my schedule to prevent me from showing up, every ounce of my being didn't want to give into the woman's demands—no matter how much honey she poured into her accent.

"I'm not sure what my schedule will be, but I can talk to my assistant and get back to you," I offered, trying to smile but managing a weak grimace.

"Oh, I'm sure you can make arrangements after I share with you the big surprise." She beckoned me closer with a wave of her finger. Leaning in with her hand up to her mouth, she whispered, "Mermaid lifeguards."

"Mermaid lifeguards!" I blurted out loud despite Pandora shushing me.

Even Amos slid off his bar stool and approached us with sudden interest. "You've got to be kidding me."

Mistletoe bobbed up and down with excitement.

"No, Miss Ashmore really did book some mermaids to act as the lifeguards for the swimming area. Although since they're all male, I guess they would be mermen."

Pandora shot her assistant a heated look, and the fairy pursed her lips shut. The event planner resumed her more pleasant countenance and patted me on my shoulder. "See? I knew I could get you to be there if I told you our big secret. When it comes to what I want, I always get my way." Her eyes flitted over to Wyatt for just a second, but they returned to me one last time. "I'll be seeing you at ten the day after tomorrow, Aurora Hart."

Stuffing her calendar back in her bag, she paused for a moment, glancing between her small floating assistant and us. She slung the carrier over her own shoulder. "Well, it was a genuine pleasure meeting all of you. I look forward to our next gathering. And Wyatt, maybe we could get together some time and talk about our home states. You know, there's this joint in Poinsettia Point that makes pretty good barbecue."

Wyatt scoffed. "Good depends entirely on what type of sauce they use. Myself, I prefer Lexington style with vinegar, ketchup, and a little spice to it."

Pandora beamed at him. "And I like mine a little thickened with a hint of peach."

"Well," I interrupted. "I'm sure you have a very busy schedule to keep, Miss Ashmore."

"Call me Pandy. All my friends do," she insisted.

"Do you need a coat or something, Miss... Pandora. I mean, Pandy?" I continued, disliking her nickname.

She waved her fingers in front of her, and a warm breeze blew around us. "Oh, I mastered a heating charm from the moment I stepped foot in the North Pole. A Southern girl like me needs some heat." Pandora dared to wink at Wyatt. "Toodles," she crooned.

Mistletoe dipped up and down in the air. "It really was good to meet you. I can't wait for you to see everything she's set up. I know you'll really love it."

"Mistletoe!" Pandora bellowed.

The fairy flapped her wings at us in goodbye and zipped off to follow her boss.

All of us Humbugs watched the two of them leave in quiet contemplation. Nutty, still perched on top of my shoulder, broke the silence.

"I like the smaller one with the wings," he said. "She seemed friendly."

"That Panda seemed nice enough. A little full of herself, but pleasant," Amos added.

"Pandy," Wyatt corrected. "And yeah, she was okay."

Rocky nodded. "I liked that she was wearing a

skirt. We don't see that very often here with all the cold and stuff."

I placed my hands on my hips. "Oh, of course you boys all liked the gorgeous girl." I pointed an accusatory finger at the lot of them. "Don't think I didn't see all of you gawking at her."

"Yeah, yeah," agreed Nutty, mimicking me with his own finger. "And she was only flirting with Wyatt, not the rest of us."

So, I hadn't been imagining the interaction between my boyfriend and the new lady. The fact that my furry roommate caught it too curdled my stomach.

"You know, I've had a long day. I think I'll head back home." I didn't even attempt to hide my disappointment.

Wyatt made his way from behind the bar and stopped me from going anywhere. He started to speak, but realized our friends leaning in to listen to us. Putting his arm around my shoulders, he guided me a little further away.

"Hey, you know I wasn't flirting with Pandora, right?" he asked.

Hearing her name come out of his mouth did nothing to change my mood. Although I knew I should be more mature about the situation, I couldn't help but feel a little petty.

"You didn't do anything to discourage her either. I

was the one who had to tell her we were dating." Even I hated myself for the slight pout on my lips as I finished my complaint.

Wyatt groaned out a long sigh and ran his fingers through his thick hair. "You know what? You're right. I got a little caught up in being around someone who reminded me of home. But that doesn't excuse the fact that I ignored you in that moment. I'm sorry, Rory."

Hearing my boyfriend say the actual words I never thought I'd hear from a guy caught me off guard and made me a little ashamed of my childish reaction.

I placed my arms around his middle and leaned into him. "No, I overreacted. I mean, she definitely had her flirt turned on, but that doesn't mean you were reciprocating."

He kissed the top of my head. "You do get that I don't see other women in that way. Only you."

I tilted my head up to see if he was being sincere. "But she was just so...put together. And me, I'm just..." I gestured at my casual appearance.

"What? Perfect?" he finished, cupping my face in his hand.

I scrunched my nose up. "I think I've got a long way to go before I reach perfect, and even then, I'm not sure I like the pressure of trying to get there. How about we use the word okay?"

It was Wyatt's turn to grimace. "That term is not going to do it. It's too generic. If you don't like me calling it like it is, then let's just say I find you perfectly imperfect."

I tapped the side of my mouth as I took a dramatic pause to mull his words over. "I think I can live with that."

He tilted my chin up with his knuckle. "As long as you're with me, then I can, too," he whispered against my lips before planting his mouth on mine.

We ignored the teasing from our fellow Humbugs for as long as possible until Wyatt broke our kiss with a slight growl in his throat. "Time to close up for the night, boys."

"But it's barely eight o'clock," groused Amos.

My boyfriend shook his head. "Maybe Clarence will let you reprobates spend time at the Wassail instead. Whatever you decide to do, you can't do it here."

"You don't have to send them home to give us privacy," I pleaded with him, watching our friends file out of the bar.

"Oh, we're leaving, too, as soon as I clean up the bar." Wyatt gathered the glasses littering the bar top and placed them on a tray.

"Where are we going?" I asked with a little confusion to this sudden change.

The bear shifter stopped what he was doing and

gave me his full attention. "I'm taking you home and then I'm gonna do my best to show you just how sorry I am."

I raised my left eyebrow at him. "And what does that entail?"

"Pizza, that British baking show you're obsessed with, and a foot massage for starters."

"And that's all?" I pressed.

He stroked his chin as if deep in thought, but the glint in his eyes hinted at fun intentions. "Maybe a few things that might get us on Santa's naughty list."

I punched the air and whooped for all I was worth. "Then I'll help you clean up so you can get to apologizing faster!"

Chapter Three

Wyatt pulled the snowmobile up to one of the pumps at the Merry Mart. I squeezed him once and unwrapped my arms from around his waist. He dismounted with ease and held out his hand to help me off the back seat of the vehicle.

"How's it going? Was the ride okay?" he asked as he lifted his goggles off his eyes.

I did the same, settling mine on top of my helmet. "As always."

He furrowed his brow. "The attached sleigh isn't making the back end wobble?"

Touching his arm for reassurance, I nodded. "It doesn't feel that much different than before. Except we're going half the speed we normally go."

Wyatt unscrewed the cap to the tank and

unhooked the handle from the pump. A small bell chimed as the energy from the Northern Lights siphoned into the vehicle bit by bit.

"Well, my backend is now a bit heavier than usual and is carrying precious cargo," he explained as he filled the tank.

I glanced back at the coolers that held the rest of the fruit from the Break Room that my boyfriend hadn't used while experimenting with potential cocktails the day before. We couldn't take too long to get to our destination for fear that the cold would spoil them.

"I'm sure Pandora's got more ingredients at the event spot." I pulled my fuzzy coat around me and shivered. "I can't wait to see how she's going to pull off a sense of summer. I mean, I get what the calendar says, but it sure doesn't feel like any summer I've been through."

The pump dinged one final time to let us know the snowmobile was full, and Wyatt replaced the nozzle in its holder. "As soon as the solstice is actually over, everything will kick into high gear for Christmas preparations. So, we'll need to enjoy it for all its worth." He pulled the zipper of my jacket up to the very top and kissed the tip of my nose. "I'm going to go in and pay Jangle, and then we can be on our way. Do you want anything from the mart?"

I settled myself on the back of the snowmobile to wait. "No, I'm good."

As I waited for him to return, I watched a mom with a small toddler pull up in front of the Fa-La-La-La-Laundromat next to the Merry Mart. She carried an overflowing basket full of clothes in her arms and struggled to open the door while also corralling her kid. When Wyatt exited the mart, he rushed over to rescue her and held the door for the little family.

"You're too sweet, you can't be real," I exclaimed when he approached.

His eyes sparkled from my compliment. "My mama raised me right."

"Such a Southern gentleman," I teased, and then sighed. "But it reminds me, I need to get over here to do some laundry soon or I'm gonna run out of things to wear."

Wyatt placed his wallet in his back pocket and pulled his gloves back on. "I told you, you're welcome to come over to my place and do laundry anytime. You don't have to use the laundromat." He pulled the goggles back over his eyes. "In fact, you'd be more than welcome to come over and stay for as long as you'd like."

My mouth dropped open and my chest tightened. "Are you...you can't be...but that's not...and it's way too soon..."

Wyatt chuckled and closed my gaping mouth with

his fingers. "Relax. I know you're not in the same place as I am, and that's perfectly fine. I was just making the offer and letting you know where I stand. You're always welcome at my place whether it's for a minute or for however long your laundry takes."

Gulping hard, I drew in a long breath. "Okay," I managed in a whisper.

He tilted his head. "Come on. I get the feeling Pandora keeps to her strict schedule with an iron fist. I'd hate to be late."

I wrapped my arms around his waist once he straddled the snowmobile again and leaned into his back while he took off. The whole journey out to the event site, I pondered the heavy meaning to Wyatt's words. He'd always been straight forward with me about how he felt, and I'd found comfort in his direct approach. But to consider moving in with him, if that's what he truly meant, was a much bigger step than I'd expected.

On one hand, my tiny place that I shared with Nutty did seem a little cramped now that I was more established in Holiday Haven than when I first came here on probation. And I made good money now that my business was thriving, so moving to a new place wouldn't strain my proverbial pocketbook. I had considered looking for a new place to rent, but it felt both exhilarating and terrifying to contemplate moving in with Wyatt. After all, we'd only been together as a couple since the Yule Ball, and that wasn't that long ago.

Scenery of Holiday Haven flew by as thoughts about my boyfriend distracted me. Wyatt drove us out of the main part of town to the outskirts based on the directions Pandora had sent both of us.

We headed down a road that took us through a dense forest. Bright light showed the way to the exit at the end of the woods, and we drove into a scene that caught both of us off guard.

Wyatt slowed down as we approached what would have been a large open field covered in snow with pines and other evergreens lining the edges. Instead of a winter landscape, a huge dome that shimmered and sparkled covered the entire space.

"Whoa." He stood up on the pedals of the snowmobile to survey the view.

"No kidding," I added, no longer focused on our relationship. "When everybody talked about a celebration, I was thinking something along the lines of the Yule Ball, but with grass hula skirts and tiki drinks."

Although the sides of the gigantic structure seemed glassy like ice, almost like a massive version of one of my sculptures, whatever it contained glistened from inside, causing occasional prisms of light to flash in the afternoon sun. I'd clearly underestimated Pandora, and that realization increased my petty jealousy of her.

Wyatt sat back down and revved the engine. "Well, we better get going if we're going to be on time."

I patted him on his back. "Can you wait one second? There's something I want to say to you."

He turned off the engine and got off the vehicle so he could look at me while I spoke.

I peeled the goggles off so I could see him while I said what was on my heart. "I'm sorry for my weird reaction to you back at the Merry Mart."

"No, you don't have to apologize. It was the completely wrong time to say anything like that, and on top of everything else, the two of us haven't had any kinds of conversations that would indicate that's where we were in our relationship. So, that's completely on me."

I couldn't help but smile at his attempt to apologize for giving me clear signals of how he felt. He really was a keeper. "Listen, I know I don't always say it, but I hope you know that I truly love you."

Happiness looked good on the guy, making him even more handsome than before. "You don't have to say it. Being with you, I can always tell."

I stood up on the snowmobile, making me just a little bit taller than him. "Good." I threw my arms

BELLA FALLS

around him and pulled him in, pressing my lips
against his.

He responded with one of his deep growls that
always warmed me from head to toe. I chuckled
against his mouth. "I love you, too, bear."

Wyatt grunted. "Say things like that, and I'll want
to keep you forever and ever." He yanked my scarf
out of the way and nibbled on my sensitive neck.

As much as I enjoyed his attention, we didn't have
time to get caught up in each other. I tugged on his
ear to get him to stop. "While I do appreciate you
inviting me to stay at your house—for however long I
choose—I don't think I'm ready for all that yet. I'm
just getting my bearings in life, and I don't want to
screw things up."

He placed his hands at the small of my back and
tugged me closer to him. "I know. Guess I'm just a bit
impatient. But you're not screwing anything up."

Old doubts from my former life floated to the
surface, and I frowned. "You didn't know me from
before. Messing things up was my specialty."

Wyatt placed his forehead against mine. "Nah,
you just hadn't learned how beautiful perfectly
imperfect looks on you."

I captured his mouth with mine one more time
before breaking away, not caring we would no longer
be on time. "You know, you're pretty cute."

He patted my behind. "Same back at you. Thank

you for clarifying things, and just know that I'm totally good with taking things at whatever speed you want. No matter what, you're kind of stuck with me."

My heart thundered as I held onto him while we closed the distance between us and the strange structure. He looped around a few other vehicles until he pulled up to what looked like the front entrance. Two large Yetis wearing sunglasses stood in front, both scowling at us.

One of them stepped forward and approached us. "You can't park here. No visitors allowed at the site."

Wyatt removed his helmet and goggles. "Pandora Ashmore invited us. We have an appointment with her at ten."

The Yeti raised a shaggy eyebrow in suspicion. "I'll have to check. Name?"

My boyfriend helped me off the back of the snowmobile. "Wyatt Berenger and Aurora Hart."

The Yeti's mouth formed a small *O*. "Aurora Hart? Not the same one who replaced Santa's sleigh?"

I wiggled my fingers at him in an intimidated greeting. "That would be me."

The Yeti whipped off his sunglasses. "Oh wow. I'm a huge fan. Hey, dude," he called out to his colleague. "You'll never guess who this is."

The other large guard lumbered over. "They shouldn't be parked here."

The first Yeti shook his hairy head. "Man, this is Aurora Hart."

"Who?" the second one asked.

"Aurora Hart. You know, the one who made a new sleigh for Santa last Christmas?" The guard who was a huge fan grunted in frustration. "It was all over the Winternet and in every single newspaper across the North Pole."

"Are they on the approved list? Because if they aren't, then it doesn't matter if she were Santa himself. Miss Ashmore told us nobody was allowed in unless they're on the list," the terse guard reiterated.

The first Yeti mouthed an apology at me. "Check for a Mr. Wyatt Berenger as well as Miss Aurora Hart."

We waited for a tense moment while the second guard passed his large finger over the list on the clipboard. "Here they are. Ten o'clock, although after all the nonsense about who she is, they're going to be late. Miss Ashmore doesn't like being thrown off her schedule."

The first Yeti pushed his colleague out of the way. "Then let me escort them inside. Do you need help carrying in the stuff you brought?" he asked us.

He and Wyatt each stacked two coolers together and lifted them as if they weighed nothing, insisting I not carry a thing. The other guard stayed outside on the watch, and the three of us approached what looked like the front of a fancy tent. Balancing the two coolers in one arm, the friendly Yeti pulled the flap open for me to enter.

The second I walked through, the entire atmosphere around me changed. Instead of the constant chill in the air that I'd become accustomed to, a blast of radiated heat hit my face. I covered my eyes with my hand to block the bright source of light beaming down on us.

"What in the world?" Wyatt exclaimed with great awe as he followed me inside.

I unwound the scarf from my neck and unzipped my puffy jacket while gawking at the scene unfolding in front of us. "How is this even possible?"

Wyatt set down his coolers and took my coat from me. "That's a complete understatement. I feel as if we walked into a tropical resort somewhere much warmer than the North Pole. The amount of magic it takes to pull this off is truly impressive."

To say what Pandora had created wasn't impressive would be a total lie. Whatever she had done to pull this off, she would solidify an incredible reputation.

Wyatt stood next to me. "I can't wait to see what adventures are going to happen next."

Chapter Four

The warmer temperature made me yearn for shorts and a light shirt rather than my typical outfit. I unzipped my dark hoodie and took it off, tying it around my jean-covered waist.

"There you are!" Mistletoe zoomed toward us, her face stiff with worry. "Pandora's been waiting for you."

Wyatt checked the time. "But we're only a couple of minutes late."

The fairy's wings quivered in agitation. "If you're five minutes early, she considers that too late. Wyatt, why don't you take all of your supplies over there to the tiki bars and get set up." She pointed a fair way away down a stone path.

"I'll help you, man, before I go back to my post."

the Yeti offered. He turned to give me a two-fingered wave. "It truly was a pleasure to meet you, Miss Hart.

"Same to you," I said with pleasant intent, realizing too late that I hadn't even caught his name. "Hey, who should I be thanking?"

The big guy smiled underneath all the shaggy hair on his face. "Name's Alfred. But you can call me Alfie."

"Thanks, Alfie." I waved at him as he helped my boyfriend take the supplies to the bar area, and then waited for the fairy assistant to explain why she floated next to me with so much agitation.

Mistletoe scrutinized my entire being with a stern glare. "You did not come prepared. I told her she should have let you know her motives for today."

I furrowed my brow in confusion. "What do you mean?"

The fairy hovered and flew in a circle around me. "No, I can't let her take advantage of you in this way. We're going to have to change up your whole look, or she'll get the upper hand. As she always does," she added under her breath.

It took me a fast second to catch on. "You mean my clothes? Why does what I'm wearing matter?"

Mistletoe looked over her shoulder with worry. "We don't have time for me to tell you everything. But I can help you out, at least for a short period." She pulled a stick out of her hair, and her green locks fell out of the coifed updo to their full length. "Have you ever been glamoured before?"

Still a little confused as to what was going on, I shook my head, watching her bob in front of me.

The assistant waved the stick in the air once, and it shimmered to life with a pale pink glow. "I'm going to help you out, but you have to promise me you won't tell Pandora." Her eyes darted back and forth as if she expected her boss to jump out of nowhere and catch her.

"I promise, but I still don't understand what you're going to do," I said.

The corner of her lip quirked up in a half smile. "Just stand still and don't move until I'm done."

Mistletoe flourished her wand in the air once before pointing it directly at me. A blast of magic hit me, but instead of pushing me down, it tickled against my skin. The clothes on my body pulsed with strange energy until they began to change. My jeans and hoodie melded together until they sparkled and changed from dark fabric to a lighter, pinker cloth. My pant legs shortened and merged into a skirt with a hem that reached right below my knees. My socks and boots disappeared, leaving my feet covered by leather sandals and my toes painted a perfect pink shade to match the fabric of my new outfit. Something knotted itself around my neck, and I dared a glance down to see the arms of a white cardigan draped around my shoulders.

"What have you done to me?" I questioned in awe.

"Trust me, you'll thank me for this later," the fairy assured me. "Now, to fix that hair."

Whenever I rode on a snowmobile, I braided my hair to keep it from blowing around. Wearing a helmet always messed it up, but for the most part, if it didn't bother Wyatt, it didn't bother me.

The tie at the bottom of the braid slid off, and the three strands unwound themselves until my hair fell free. Feeling as if a brush, a blow dryer, and a curling iron attacked my head at the same time, it took a few more seconds until the sensation ceased.

"And finally, how about a little makeup to finish the look." Mistletoe circled the tip of her wand around my face. "Nothing too artificial. Just a little boost to your natural beauty."

A pleasant breeze with a slightly floral scent blew against my skin, and it felt as if I wore a refreshing face mask. Although Vail had been teaching me how to use makeup for everyday use, I still preferred to wear only a little bit of lip gloss most of the time. The magical wind died away, and Mistletoe hovered away from me, observing her handiwork.

"There. Now, you look perfect." With one final flourish of her wand, a mirror appeared.

I gawked at the pretty young woman reflected back at me. She wore a pink dress with a tropical flower print on it. The cardigan tied at the neck gave her a more professional than casual look, but the whole ensemble definitely fit in with the warm weather of the special environment.

Mistletoe worked her hair back into a bun and stuck the wand into it to hold it up. She placed a finger on her lips to remind to keep her secret and tipped her head to her right.

"And here is our guest of honor for today's sneak preview. I'm sure all of you remember Miss Aurora Hart." Pandora walked in our direction, followed by a large group.

Her smile seemed friendly enough, but the gleam in her eyes resembled that of a big cat looking at its soon-to-be-eaten prey. However, when she registered my outfit and how I looked, her gaze turned downright frosty.

A few cameras turned in my direction as a couple of flashes peppered the air. A familiar face pushed its way to the front to stand next to Pandora. "Miss Hart, Merry Mittens here. It's so nice to see you doing so well after your triumph during last year's Seasonal Spirit Awards. What do you think of this new event Pandora and her team have put together?"

Voice recorders and more cameras pointed right

at me. Panicked butterflies took flight in my stomach, and my palms began to sweat. "Uh, I've just arrived, but I can say that I never expected something this spectacular right here in Holiday Haven."

The Winternet reporter followed her question with another one. "One of the perks of winning the Seasonal Spirit Awards in all of the North Pole was this giant celebration. Your whole town has you to thank for it."

My cheeks heated with embarrassment. "I think everybody in the town already contributed their very best to the awards, so really the win is due to everyone's contributions."

Merry Mittens nodded her head. "But it was *you* who solved the mystery of what happened to Santa's original sleigh."

I pointed at myself. "I didn't do it alone. There were many of my friends who assisted in finding the culprit, and I'm glad that every one of them, plus all who participated in the SSA's, will get to enjoy such a beautiful environment." A trickle of sweat rolled down the side of my face, and I had to fight not to wipe it away.

Several of the reporters shouted out questions, and Pandora's expression turned from satisfaction to consternation. Whatever her plan had been to catch me off guard, she was beginning to realize that ambushing me with a bunch of reporters wasn't bringing her the attention she desired.

Waving a hand in the air, she called their attention, emphasizing her Southern accent. "Yoohoo, everybody. Let's not overwhelm my guest with too many questions." She sauntered over to me and threw her arm around my shoulders as if we were best friends. "After all, the two of us do what we do not for ourselves but for the good of others, isn't that right, Rory?"

My lips hurt from holding my tense smile. "Sure, Pandora."

"Oh, sugar," she crooned, leaning into me. "How many times do I have to remind you to call me Pandy?" She turned her attention to a small gnome who stood next to Merry Mittens. "Because we're such good friends."

The gnome stroked his long white beard. "How long have the two of you known each other?"

Sharp nails dug into my bare arm as Pandora squeezed me tight. I searched my brain for a quick lie just to get things over with faster. "For all the time I've known her, she's been an absolute character."

The event planner giggled like a young girl. "Oh, you are such a tease."

Someone from the back shouted over the rest, "So, Miss Ashmore, you've shown us this amazing beach bubble that you created, complete with a sandy beach, a sparkling ocean with water and waves, and lots of neat ways to have fun in the sun. How did you manage to pull all of this off?"

Pandora dropped her arm and maneuvered her body in front of mine. Clasping her hands together, she addressed the crowd of reporters with an even sharper accent. "Well, I can't give away all my secrets, but let's just say that it took lots of planning and a whole lot of my special charms to get things just right." With a flourish of her fingers, a few sparkles framed her entire body.

A short man in disheveled clothes with a camera slung around his neck elbowed people out of the way until he stood at the very front. "Aurora, it's no secret that you were seen dancing and kissing a certain somebody at your local Yule Ball. Are you still together?"

Caught off guard with the subject of the question, I swallowed hard, not sure what answer to give him. "I'm not sure how that's relevant to the solstice celebration." More sweat beaded on my upper lip.

The corners of the reporter's mouth quirked up, and he licked his lips. "If you haven't figured it out, you're kind of a celebrity, Miss Hart. Believe me, our readers are more than interested in your love life."

It was somebody just like him who had snuck a picture of Wyatt and I smooching on the balcony at the Yule Ball and posted it in one of the gossip rags.

With the relationship so new, it didn't really bother me at the time. But now that my boyfriend and I seemed to be in a period of potential transition into something even more serious, I didn't want to involve the public.

"Let's just say that I'm off the dating market," I said, hoping that would be enough.

Someone else quipped from the middle of the pack, "That only gives us a partial answer."

I raised one eyebrow. "You noticed," I joked, following up with a laugh.

Merry Mittens chuckled with me and nodded in approval, and several of the other reporters followed suit. I held my breath, wishing I could melt away or dig myself a hole in the sand and disappear.

Pandora blocked her guests' view of me. "Besides, I invited y'all here to feature my special solstice celebration."

Merry raised her hand. "One more question for Aurora, if I may?"

Pandora nodded, but I heard her declare under her breath, "If you must."

I trained my eyes on the friendlier Winternet reporter. "Of course."

"With Santa's new sleigh such a big hit, will you be contributing a special sculpture for the solstice festivities?" she asked. The gaggle of reporters quieted down, and they all stood in anticipatory silence, waiting.

Pandora tittered and took a step back to stand next to me again. "Oh, don't you think Rory should just attend as a guest and enjoy herself?"

The gnome raised his pencil in the air. "Actually, I would think you'd want to commission an ice sculpture from Miss Hart. After all, who wouldn't want the maker of Santa's sleigh to create something that could be a centerpiece for all to admire? Maybe something that people could take Elfies with on their spell phones."

"But you're missing one important thing—I make *ice* sculptures. Who knows how it would react to whatever makes this bubble so warm?" I worried. "I think there's already lots for people to admire."

Pandora's eyes flashed to mine, and the same predatory gleam she'd possessed before returned. "You know what? I think it's a marvelous idea."

"You do?" I asked, caught off guard once again.

She clapped her hands together in giddy glee. "I'm almost cross that I didn't think of it myself. We've got a few more days before the celebration, which should be more than enough time for you to create something truly original and spectacular." Raising her hand in the air, she commanded everyone's attention. "You heard it right here from me first. The summer solstice celebration will feature an original Aurora Hart sculpture."

Pandora slid her arm through mine and turned me left and right to pose for pictures. No matter what she said or how wide she smiled, something deep inside me doubted her motives. I also disliked being forced into doing something just because she placed me in a position where it was impossible to say no.

"Don't worry, honey," she said as she posed with me. "I'm sure everything will turn out perfectly."

Chapter Five

My jaws and cheeks hurt after faking a smile for the last few minutes of pictures and footage of Pandora and me. Despite my desire to run away far and fast, I stuck it out and braved every flash and final question. Of course, the event planner soaked up every ounce of the attention, interpreting my uncomfortable silence as permission to speak for me. By the end of it all, not only was I committed to creating what sounded like a massive sculpture to be placed somewhere prominent, I now had to come up with a few smaller pieces to be scattered around the entire event space.

My brain overloaded with the sheer amount of work ahead of me in such a short time on top of being cornered into having to agree to it all in front of the reporters. I didn't even notice that Pandora had ended the interviews until a few of them thanked me for my time as they followed her toward the exit.

Merry Mittens stayed behind the rest of her colleagues. She placed a sympathetic hand on my shoulder. "I've been doing this job long enough to know when someone is surprised."

I snorted. "Guess I'm not that good of an actor." Realizing who I'd just admitted that to, I covered my mouth.

She squeezed my shoulder and let me go. "Don't worry, this is completely off the record. I just wanted to say I'm sorry if I contributed to this awkward spectacle. But if it's any consolation, after what you pulled off with the sleigh, I think you'll have no problem in creating something for this event." Merry glanced at someone behind me. "Guess I'm being given the boot for now. See you later, and good luck."

The reporter's sympathy helped me feel a little more justified in the inner panic that was threatening to unleash itself on my entire being. I glanced around, trying to figure out what I should do. Should I run after the crowd of reporters and tell them I couldn't do it? Maybe I could find another exit and slink away? Or maybe I should sit down right where I was and have a full-on meltdown. I covered my face, not even able to decide on what to do next.

Strong hands caressed my bare arms. "Hey, what's wrong?" Wyatt asked.

I crashed into his massive chest and buried myself in his warm embrace. "You have no idea what just happened."

He rubbed my back. "Then why don't you tell me."

Without taking a breath, I told him all about Pandora ambushing me with the reporters, explaining the details except one. It occurred to me as I drew comfort from his touch that telling him I hadn't been straight about our relationship might hurt his feelings.

When I finished, Wyatt hugged me tighter and kissed the top of my head. "That sounds very overwhelming. And you know you don't have to go through with it. If Pandora's any kind of professional, then she'll understand that since you hadn't agreed to this beforehand or signed a contract, then she can't hold you to it."

His revelation startled me. In my alarm, I hadn't thought about the logistics of the entire scenario. Cora usually took care of contracts and stuff, leaving me the space to be the artist. So, maybe I could get my own assistant involved, and she could make it clear I couldn't possibly commit to such a big task at the last minute.

Seeing the loophole eased some of my tension. I

squeezed my boyfriend one more time and pulled back so I could look up at him. "You seem to say all the right things."

Wyatt brushed a stray tear off my cheek. "Good, because you looked pretty shaken up there. But can I ask you one thing?"

"Sure."

He took one step away from me while his eyes roamed up and down my body. "Tell me how you went from jeans and a hoodie to all of that?"

I'd forgotten all about Mistletoe's glamour. That fairy had earned herself a big present for truly saving me. "What, this old thing?" I joked in a bad fake Southern accent while giving the skirt of the dress a little twirl.

Wyatt's eyes flashed brighter with appreciation. "I mean, I'm not saying I don't like it. Just can't figure out how it happened."

"Yoo-hoo!" Pandora sang out from nearby. "Just the bartender I've been lookin' for."

I put my finger over my lips to keep him from saying anything else. "I'll tell you later," I insisted with a whisper.

The event planner threw a little extra swing into her step as she approached. When she reached us, she barely acknowledged my presence. Again. "Well, what do you think?"

Too much of a gentleman, Wyatt didn't pull out

of her clutches. "I have to admit, the whole thing is pretty amazing. I can tell you, everybody in Holiday Haven will be incredibly impressed. You'll definitely make your mark."

"Well, thank you for such a wonderful compliment, kind sir," Pandora called out with her lilting accent. "I must say, it feels good when all my plans come through, including getting the two of you here so I can show off my creation."

Pandora's ability to seem so pleasant while being completely dismissive impressed and irritated me. When she dared to snake her arm through Wyatt's, I leaned more towards irritation. Nothing would please me more than throwing a wrench in her machinations.

"By the way, Pandy," I said, putting extra emphasis on using her nickname. "I'll have to run everything by my assistant to see if it's even possible for me to sculpt anything for the event."

The planner stopped giving my boyfriend an unnatural amount of attention, her eyes snapping in my direction. "What do you mean? I thought it was a done deal."

"Well, I'm sure you're well aware that work of that magnitude should be discussed well ahead of time. And as we don't have any signed contracts…" I hoped she'd let the whole thing drop.

Her dark-stained bottom lip jutted out in a

perfect pout. "Oh, but we're friends, aren't we Rory? And your word's as good as a handshake to me." She waved the whole thing off. "I'm sure whatever you come up with will be just fine. But now that it'll be out in the press, you won't want to give anything but your best. After all, while you've had favorable coverage since last Christmas, it only takes one slip up for your whole reputation to come crashing down."

My loophole evaporated with her observations. Because the whole idea was solidified in front of the reporters, there really wasn't a way to back out of it without tarnishing my good name. Pandora had won this particular round, whether I wanted her to or not.

I blew out a breath of frustration in an attempt to regroup. "Fine. I think I can come up with something."

Pandora looked down her nose at me in self-satisfaction as she kept a grip on Wyatt's arm. "You'll make so many people happy." Her tone changed in a flash as she tapped her finger at the side of her mouth. "Although now that you mention it, I do hope that the heating spell I've charmed over the whole place won't affect your ice. Oh dear, maybe in my utter enthusiasm, I have made a potential mess for you."

"Wouldn't it be a mess for us?" I pointed out.

"Well," she drew out, "I think it would reflect

more on you than me since it would be a failure of your work."

Wyatt unhooked her hand from his arm and moved away to stand next to me. "I'm sure Rory will do her absolute best."

Pandora's eyes narrowed for a split second before she covered her reaction with her signature tittering giggle. "Of course, I didn't mean to imply anything else. Now, I'm eager to try all of the drinks you've created and choose the best ones to have my staff serve at the celebration."

Wyatt captured my hand in his. "Wait until you try the Fire and Ice. I think I've gotten the recipe just right." He pulled me along with him in the direction of the bar, and my smugness level maxed out as we passed the party planner.

Pandora emitted a loud exhale and caught up, working her way in between my boyfriend and me. "Oh, I think maybe Rory would benefit from exploring the whole beach bubble. See if she can find some inspiration for what she's going to create while I sample this fine drink of yours." She pushed forward until it became awkward for Wyatt and me to continue holding hands.

With regret, I let go of him. He flashed me an apologetic look, and I gave him a slight shake of my head to convey that I knew who was to blame.

"She's right. I should look around to see if

anything will spark an idea." My words tasted like ash, knowing that her suggestion actually was a good one. I just wished I had come up with it first.

Knowing she'd won again, Pandora glowed under the beach bubble sun. "If you have any problems, be sure to let Mistletoe know. Although I suspect she's already helped you out at least once today." She eyed me up and down. "By the way, hon, *love* your outfit. Bless your heart, that color is almost flattering on you."

Heat ignited in my veins, and a buzz of energy crackled inside of me. If I lost control, there was no telling what I might melt, including that sinister smile on the planner's lips.

"I think it makes your eyes sparkle," Wyatt said to draw attention to him. He widened his eyes in warning.

I clenched my fists to contain my magic and counted to ten in my head. "Thanks, sweetie. A compliment like that will get you anywhere with me." My eyebrows wiggled with purposeful intent.

"Aw, how precious," Pandora exclaimed with mock enthusiasm. "Come on, Wyatt. I'm absolutely parched. We'll see you later, Rory." She pulled my boyfriend away with her, walking closer to him than a casual acquaintance should.

Before they could get too far, I thought of one

request I could demand. "Hey, Pandy, one more thing."

She stopped mid-stride. "What's that, sugar?" she asked without turning to face me.

"You know, since the request for my work has come so late, I could really use some help." I smirked as I pushed. "I'd like to bring in my friends to help me out, especially since I'll be working so hard to get things done in time for the opening day."

Now Pandora was the one in the hot seat. If she told me no, she'd look bad in front of Wyatt.

Unable to weasel her way out, she turned around and replaced the obvious scowl on her face with a tolerant half-grin. "When you say 'friends,' how many are you talking? We are trying to keep a lid on things here to maintain the maximum amount of surprise."

I counted the Humbugs in my head and included my faithful assistant. "Six."

"I'll give you four," Pandora countered.

"Done!" I exclaimed before she could take it back. Now the score between us stood at one to one, even.

An audible sigh escaped her lips and her body stiffened. "Please be sure to give the names of your guests to one of the guards before you leave. And keep it to those people only. If one of them can't make it, I don't want you substituting someone else."

Pandora smirked at me. "You know, I'm surprised you need any help at all since I thought it was a one-woman show. None of the publicity you earned mentioned anybody else."

The woman thought she'd try to take the one point I'd earned away from me, but I could give just as good as I got. "Funny, I'm pretty sure you didn't list out everyone involved in making this entire event space work."

She placed an indignant hand on her hip. "You don't name the hired help. That's their job, to be invisible."

"Oh, the people I'll be bringing are my friends. But without them, I wouldn't have anything. I guess that's the difference." I wondered if she had any friends at all if spoke to others the way she did to me. I shrugged as if the conversation meant nothing. "Don't let me keep you any longer."

Wyatt failed to stifle a chuckle while standing behind Pandora, and when she whipped around to face him, he covered it up by coughing into his hand.

"Let's go, Mr. Berenger," she groused, grabbing his arm and pulling him away.

I watched the two of them disappear as the stone path toward the bar curved around a group of potted hibiscus plants. My creative brain interrupted my growing disdain for the event planner. Maybe I could do a large sculpture that featured all kinds of tropical plants and flowers? But part of the natural beauty of the flora was their fantastic colors, and other than the magical glow from inside the ice that came from my magic, I wouldn't be able to pull off bright hues.

Kicking a little pebble with my sandaled foot, I wandered away from the stone path, not exactly sure where I'd end up. I struggled to walk through the soft sand, the tops of it warmed by the bright sun shining above us. Beads of sweat formed on my forehead, and I stopped in sudden dread. What if my sculptures really couldn't stand up to the heat? I'd never had to test that possibility while living and working in the North Pole district. And if my sculptures did melt in this special environment, then I was sure that would make the news headlines.

"Excuse me, are you one of the staff?" a squeaky voice asked me.

I turned to face the speaker but had to look down at the sandy floor below. A bird with gray-white feathers, orange webbed feet, and a large bill with a dangling wattle stood in front of me. The pelican wore a white scarf with a red border tied around its neck and a sailor cap on top of its head.

"No. Well, yes, I guess I kind of do. You know, I'm not exactly sure," I rambled.

"Oh, that's very noncommittal. I need some help carrying boxes to the souvenir shop and can't find anybody that's not already busy doing other things." The bird clacked its beak in frustration.

"I'd be happy to help you..." I gave him the space to introduce himself.

"Bill. Well, for this event, I'm supposed to be Barnacle Bill and dress up with an eye patch and black hat with a feather. But I found this cap and scarf in the costume box and thought I could convince the person in charge to let me wear them instead," the pelican answered, beckoning me to follow him to a large stack of boxes stashed near a tall post with arrows pointing to different areas of the event space.

After introducing myself, I grabbed a few of the lighter boxes and stacked them together before picking them up. "I like what you're wearing right now. But from my interactions with Pandora, I'm pretty sure she'll want exactly what she asked for."

Bill led me back onto the stone path and walked me toward the straw huts lining one side of the beach bubble. "Oh, not the person who acts like she's in charge. I mean the person who's really running things."

I pondered his reply as we followed the path until we came to a hut with a painted sign that read *Barnacle Bill's Bounty*. The pelican placed his box down and opened the side door.

"You can put those down there, and I'll get them inside," he offered.

"What did you mean by the person who's really in charge?" I asked, a little confused. "I thought Pandora Ashmore put this whole thing together."

The pelican waved his wing in front of his gaping bill. "I really shouldn't have said anything. Please forget you ever heard that. But let's just say, there's a difference between those that squawk the loudest and those who make things happen, if you know what I mean."

If Pandora wasn't the actual person who got things done, then who was? That little mystery intrigued me, but I didn't want to make the pelican too uncomfortable in case he could be a source for information later.

I helped him get the rest of the boxes into his hut. "What kinds of souvenirs are you selling?"

"Oh, I've got a lot of this and that." He opened one of his boxes. "There are some shell necklaces and earrings I'll have to put on display. And some neon-rimmed sunglasses. And of course, straw hats." Taking his sailor hat off, he placed a wide-brimmed hat on his head that was so big it covered his eyes.

I chuckled at the absurd bird until an idea dawned on me. "Hey, may I buy a hat and some sunglasses?"

Bill took off the hat and placed it on the counter.

"You can have this one and pick out a pair that you like on me. Call it payment for your help."

"Thanks." I took the hat and chose a neon pink pair of glasses. "I truly appreciate it, Barnacle Bill."

The pelican's beak widened into a smile. "You're welcome. Guess I'll see you around, Rory."

"I'll definitely be back," I promised.

As I trekked away, thoughts of what I might use the souvenirs for battled my brain for attention with trying to figure out exactly who Bill was talking about. I walked off the stone path and back out onto the sand. If I wanted to conduct an experiment, I needed to do it where the temperature would be at its hottest.

Choosing a blue-and-white striped changing tent as my landmark, I steadied myself, taking in a few deep breaths and listening to the sound of waves crashing to center myself.

Once I felt calm and prepared, I activated my magic and allowed ice to form layer by layer until I had a decent-sized ice chunk that stood a little wider than me and came up to my chin. Mixing my fire magic with my ice powers, I melted and solidified the ice until it fashioned into an easy, three-tiered figure that any resident in Holiday Haven would recognize.

I finished the carrot nose of my ice snowman and stood back to admire the simple character. Taking the hat, I placed it on the frozen head of my test subject. I balanced the sunglasses on its carrot nose and stood back to assess my work.

"Well, I'll know tomorrow if this will melt into a giant disaster or if I can beat that smug planner at her own game."

Chapter Six

Rocky took the hit and volunteered to be one of the Humbugs not to come to the beach bubble. According to him, he wanted to be surprised with the rest of the town. However, I highly suspected the newest book from one of his favorite romance authors releasing today had more to do with him giving up his spot with such ease.

Cora wanted to join us so she could give Pandora a piece of her mind over how poorly she treated me. Feeling that the interaction might land me in hotter water, I encouraged her to stay behind and reschedule some of the appointments for the rest of the week.

I rode with Wyatt again, this time enjoying the

faster ride since we weren't pulling a sleigh ladened with supplies. Instead of hugging my boyfriend tight as I rode, I held onto the side handles to stay on so I wouldn't crush Nutty, who had crawled inside my puffy coat to stay warm on the journey.

Amos rode right behind us with Vale as his passenger. It had surprised all of us that the older man wanted to join since he seemed to hate everything in life, especially anything new. But when we'd teased him about it, he'd shut us all up by telling us that the beach had been Mabel's favorite place to vacation.

When we exited the edge of the woods and burst into the clearing, Wyatt led the way toward the carpeted entrance again. Only this time, there wasn't any snow to drive the vehicles over. He aimed us a little further away and parked as close as possible. Clarence met us by the two Yeti guards.

"How did you get here before us?" Vale asked.

The pub owner stood a little straighter. "I'm a vampire."

Nutty popped his head out of the top of my coat. "Yeah, yeah, I'll bet he changed into a bat or something to get here faster."

Clarence snickered at my roommate's assumption. "Not quite, although I appreciate the lore that led you to that deduction, my furry friend. But I can move faster than most beings. Definitely quicker than your clunky vehicles." He sniffed once to end the conversation.

I counted all of us and came up with five. "But don't we have too many?"

The unpleasant guard tapped the clipboard with names. "If you're not on here, then you're not coming in."

Alfie nudged his colleague with his hip. "Oh, come on. It'll be fine."

"No, rules are rules." The Yeti crossed his arms. "And if you don't comply with them, then I'll report you to the boss."

"And would that boss be Miss Ashmore or somebody else?" I inquired.

Alfie avoided my gaze, but the other guard answered with stony silence.

Wyatt clapped Clarence on the shoulder. "I arranged for my friend here to be my plus one to help with the bar setup."

It pleased me to know that my boyfriend pushed Pandora's boundaries as well. "Are you going to be selling some of your Holid-Ale?" I asked the pub owner.

"In fact, I had already brewed some pale ale in honor of the solstice. I sent some kegs of it over to the site yesterday," the vampire replied.

"So, maybe you could call it Pale Holid-Ale," I suggested.

"Could we please get everybody checked in so we can keep the front clear?" the unpleasant guard insisted, interrupting our banter.

He grunted as he checked each person off, and Alfie escorted all of us in like he had the day before. "I'm sorry. My colleague is a little crankier than usual today because he says he's too hot."

The rest of us removed our coats and loose coverings since I'd warned them about the huge shift in temperature. And I couldn't rely on Mistletoe to glamour me a more appropriate outfit this time.

I pulled off my sweatpants to reveal a pair of shorts underneath. "It does feel a little warmer than it did yesterday. And what happened to the snow out in front?"

Alfie scratched his shaggy head. "I'm not exactly sure. When we arrived for our shift this morning, it was just gone." He wiped his arm across his forehead. "Woo, it's quite balmy inside."

Nutty picked up a tiny piece of broken-off palm frond and fanned himself with it. "At least all of you can shed your heavier layers. I can't step out of my fur."

"How about you all come with me to the tiki bar, and I'll set you up with some frosty drinks," Wyatt offered.

Amos checked the nonexistent watch on his arm. "Ain't it a little early in the day to be drinking? I mean, for the rest of you. I'm retired, so I can drink anytime I want."

"You still have Pine & Dandy to run," I reminded him.

He scratched his grizzled chin. "Only when I want to. Now, enough about my daily schedule. Let's get us some cold drinks." He shaded his eyes. "I wish I'd brought my sunglasses."

I waved a finger in the air. "I know a place we can get some."

After we all picked out some sunglasses at Barnacle Bill's hut and paid for them, Wyatt hooked us up with some drinks. Amos chose to take a seat at the tiki bar to stay with my boyfriend and Clarence. Vale, Nutty, and I went on a mission to find the blue-and-white striped changing tent where I'd left my experiment. Based on how high the temperature had risen, I estimated I'd find my summer snowman in a puddle.

Nutty scampered ahead of us, picking up seashells along the way, as I caught Vale up on everything that had happened to land me in my current predicament. "So, you had to agree, otherwise you would have looked bad in front of all the reporters. That Pandora sounds crafty."

"I mean, I guess others find that Southern accent charming, but every time I hear her giggle, I just want to..." I pictured tripping her or pulling her hair out of its perfect coif. "Well, let's just say that I don't think we'll end up best friends after she's packed up and gone back home."

Vale smirked at me. "I thought you liked a Southern accent?"

"Correction. I like Wyatt's," I specified. "And his grandpappy's. Beyond that, Pandora's the only other person from that region that I've spoken to at any length."

Nutty scurried in our direction. "I think I found what you're looking for." He bounced in place as if the sand hurt his paws.

I asked if he wanted to ride on my shoulder, and he took me up on my offer, clambering up my legs and torso faster than I could pick him up. He directed me which way to go until I spotted the tent. To my surprise, I also caught the sun reflecting off a glistening ice sculpture.

"Huh, I guess my magic is more special than I thought." I ran my hands over the surface of the ice and found it smooth rather than watery.

Vale bent down to look at the sand around the base of the snowman. "I'll be honest, I'm only seeing a little bit of wet sand at the bottom. Not much at all. Perhaps if you adjusted your ratio of ice, it would be completely unmeltable. Is that even a word?"

"Hey, I'm impressed it's held up under this heat like it has. Since I'm still learning about my abilities and am still pretty new at my job, I was really worried," I admitted.

"Yeah, yeah, I heard you pacing around our place a lot last night. I almost got up to offer you some of my nuts." Nutty petted the side of my face to comfort me.

My squirrel roommates almost-offering of his favorite thing in the world warmed my heart. I kissed the tip of his tiny nose, and he busied himself grooming his face.

Vale adjusted the straw hat on the top of her head and pushed her bright blue sunglasses up her nose. "Since you know it works, what do you think you'd like to sculpt today?"

With my vagabond past, I didn't really have any experience being in a tropical setting. "I don't know. What kinds of things make you think summer and beach?"

My best friend shrugged. "I've never really been anywhere other than a few towns over."

"You've never traveled that far outside of Holiday Haven?" I apologized for the tone of utter shock in my voice.

"I've always loved it here. Why would I want to

travel if I'm happiest right where I am? Although, if there are places like this, maybe I've sold myself short." She buried her feet in the sand. "You know, it's cooler once you get a little further down."

"Let's walk around and see if anything pops out," I suggested.

The three of us walked the perimeter of the beach. We passed several lounge chairs set up in rows in front of the changing tents. A large straw hut sat in the middle of things, and when we checked its contents, we found rafts, floats, and beach toys ready to be used.

The sound of music floated through the air, and we followed it until we came across someone with broad shoulders and dark hair pulled back into a loose bun sitting on the edge of a rock that jutted out into the water. Whoever it was strummed a small instrument.

"Excuse me, but that music is pretty. What's that you're playing?" I asked.

The figure scooted on the edge of the rock, and a man with tan skin and dark markings wrapped around his right bicep, covering his entire left forearm, greeted us. When he turned sideways, his lower half shaped like a fish fin followed, glistening green and blue.

"Aloha, my friends. I'm glad you liked what you heard." He held out his smallish guitar. "This is my ukulele. I was just strumming it a bit to pass the time."

"Oh my stars, are you one of the famed mermaid lifeguards?" Vale gushed.

"I am." He strummed a couple of chords. "The name's Makai. Me and my sister were hired all the way from our home off the island of Oahu. There are a few more of my kind from other places here as well. Wanna take my picture?" He flexed his massive arms to show his muscles.

Nutty held onto my ear to keep his balance. "What are those markings on your skin?"

"These are my traditional kākau, tapped into my skin during many a kā uhi by a great kahuna." Makai's flex turned into an opportunity to show off his markings. "He chose the design based on my story and my moʻokūʻauhau."

"That means our family lineage," a woman who looked very much like Makai said as her head emerged from the water next to where he sat. "You can't resist showing off in front of new people, can you? I must apologize for my brother. He's always been a bit of a showoff."

"Shut up, Kailani," the big guy gritted through his teeth. "Besides, I was showing them my ukulele."

Vale giggled. "Is that what you call your muscles?"

"I knew it!" his sister exclaimed. "See? Showoff."

A gray fin broke the surface, and I jumped back

even though I was nowhere close to it. "Look out! There's a shark by you!"

Kailani turned her attention to the water behind her but scoffed. "We're not afraid of sharks, but that's definitely not one of them. This is our friendly nai'a." She grabbed onto the fin, and a bottle-nosed face broke the surface of the water.

"Aw, it's a dolphin," I gushed. "I've never seen one in person."

"Its name is Nai'a?" Vale asked.

"No, that's what we call a spinner dolphin in our language. Her name is Hina, named after the mo'o sea goddess. Because she's so pretty. Yes, you are, aren't you?" She rubbed the dolphin under its chin, and it chittered at her.

Makai dangled his fin over the water. "Oh yeah, well, your dolphin isn't as cute as my honu." He put his fingers to his lips and blew out a shrill whistle.

The water stirred around a dark figure that surfaced, and a small head popped up. When it saw who called it, the creature rose in the water until its whole shell shone in the bright sun.

"This is Koa. He's a green sea turtle. Someday, he'll outlive all of us, but he's in his twenties right now," Makai explained.

"How do you know how old he is?" Nutty asked. "Do you count all the spots on his face and fins?"

My squirrel roommate's question caused the big

guy to almost fall off the rock from all his laughter. "No, my friend. Because I was just barely five when I greeted him in the water for the first time. You know, they start off very small and have to fight their way to the water when they come out of their shell."

"They have to crack it open, like a nut?" My furry friend risked singeing his feet and scrambled down so he could stand at the surf to get a closer look.

As if equally as curious, Koa pushed his way through the water until he floated right on the edge in front of Nutty.

"Maybe not as tough as a nut, but yes, he had to fight his way out of the shell and across the sand without being picked off by predators. Our parents brought me and Kailani to watch those who were strong enough make it to the water." Makai looked down at the turtle with a lot of affection. "And he definitely was tough, so I named him after the hardwood native to our islands, Koa. It's what my instrument is made from, too."

He strummed a few more chords, and I marveled at how unlikely it seemed to meet new friends all the way from Hawaii.

Makai emitted a quieter short whistle, and Koa swam over to him. "As soon as he made it into the water, he swam right up to me and stopped. Just stared into my eyes, as if he knew me. Ever since then, we've been best friends."

A splash of water hit Makai in the face. "I thought I was your best friend," Kailani teased.

"If I weren't holding my ukulele, I would so get you back, kaikaina," he threatened with a mischievous grin. "But there's always later, and you'll never know when it's coming."

"Did he just call you a bad name?" I asked.

Kailani chortled. "No, that just means little sister." She whispered something to the dolphin, and the sea animal swam closer to the rock. It flipped out of the water and swam backwards, splashing its tail so that loads of water doused her brother.

Makai shook out his long, wavy hair from the messy bun. "Here, will one of you look after this for me?" He held out his ukulele.

I rushed over and climbed onto the rock so I could hold the instrument. "Is it okay if I give it back to you in a little bit? We need to keep exploring first."

"Perfectly fine," Makai answered. "And I'll teach you how to play it. But right now, I have to teach my little sister a much-needed lesson."

He rolled off the rock into the water, and the two of them splashed about until they both dove under, their tails slapping the surface to propel them.

I held onto the small wooden instrument with great care as Vale, Nutty, and I moved along the shoreline until we reached the edge of the beach bubble.

"I think I have a good idea for the sculpture," I told my friends. "But I'm trying to figure out how to pull it off before I start."

"Does it involve two mermaids?" Vale teased.

"Maybe."

"And a honu?" Nutty added.

"Perhaps." I smiled at our game.

Vale bumped against me. "And Hina?"

I hit my head with the palm of my hand. "Now you see why my idea might be insane." My brain tried to work out how I could feature all four things and give them life like I just saw them.

My half elf friend grabbed my arm. "Do you hear something?"

Nutty scampered off in front of us and disappeared through some fronds. After a moment, his head popped out of the leaves, and he crooked his tiny finger to beckon us closer. We went over and crouched down to hide so we could eavesdrop.

Two people argued from behind the palmetto palms. The deeper voice said, "I don't know what the boss was thinking. If we try to make it any hotter, it'll take the entire system down."

A high-pitched voice answered back. "You heard what was asked for. Make it all melt or we'll be in trouble."

"But the magic is running at its full capacity. If we tamper with it anymore, it could put the whole place and everybody in it at risk. Plus, did you see what was happening on the outside?" the deep voice asked, unable to hide his tone of concern.

"Our job is to take care of things on the inside. We're not paid enough to consider what happens outside of the dome," the higher-pitched voice hissed. "Here."

I heard a slight groan as something was being given to the other worker.

"Add these at the base of the source," the one making demands said. "Make sure to bury them underneath. That should do the trick."

A short pause followed, and I assumed the other worker inspected what they'd been handed.

"The instructions we were given were very clear. We weren't to touch anything," the deeper voice said.

"Don't make me go get the boss because you know how unhappy it will make her. And if she's unhappy, then I am." The higher voice gritted, "And then I'll make sure you and all of your team are unhappy as well."

"I already am," groaned the deep voice.

"Just get it done," the high-pitched figure demanded.

I held my breath, worried that whoever it was would spot us. Vale, Nutty, and I stayed quiet until we heard the grumbling fade away as whoever was on the receiving end left in the opposite direction.

Vale stood up and brushed the sand off her clothes. "What do you suppose that was about?"

I straightened to my full height, all thoughts about my sculpture replaced by concern. "I have an inkling, but I'm afraid to voice it out loud, just in case it's true."

"Say it so I can see if it's what I think it is," my friend insisted.

I took a deep breath and then blurted out my theory. "I think that the increase in temperature isn't a mistake. It's intentional, and whoever wants it to happen doesn't care if it's causing things to go wrong."

"Ooh, like the snow all melted away and stuff at the entrance," Nutty added.

"Exactly," I agreed.

"But there's a bigger problem, isn't there?" Vale grimaced. "It sounds like whoever's in charge wants it even hotter for some reason."

"To melt something. Surely, that can't mean they want all the people who are working in here to suffer?" I shook my head. "That doesn't make sense."

Vale gasped. "Are they talking about Pandora wanting all of this?"

I hadn't even thought about who they meant when they were saying the boss wanted things hotter. But according to Bill, there were two different people in charge. One who said that they were in charge and one who actually was the boss.

"I don't know, but if things are going as wrong as it seems, then we need to find out how and why," I said, glancing at my two friends. "Before things get even worse."

Chapter Seven

The three of us stopped exploring for inspiration and made our way back to where we'd met Makai and Kailani. I gave the male mermaid back his ukulele with a brief thanks before returning to the stone path.

Vale, Nutty, and I got a little lost as the path took us through different areas that included food vendors, more souvenir shops, a photo booth, and other fun ways to remember the event.

The more staff we passed, the more the back of my neck heated and my nose itched. My eyes darted around, trying to figure out why, and I caught a few people staring at me. When they saw me looking at them, they'd quickly get busy doing something else. Several staff whispered to each other while watching me walk with my friends.

"I'm pretty sure I'm being watched," I hissed at Vale and Nutty.

"Yeah, yeah," my roommate agreed. "They're definitely paying a lot of attention to you."

"But that's not totally unusual," Vale countered. "Rory tends to get a lot of attention."

I loved how my friend's kind soul always gave everyone the benefit of the doubt. "Maybe right after the sleigh thing. For the most part, nobody's bothered by me." I turned my head and caught a couple of pixies hovering in the air right behind us, trying to listen in on our conversation. "But this is downright weird."

We followed the signs to the tiki bar, and a sense of relief flooded my entire being when I spotted Wyatt teaching some of the staff how to make one of his drinks. Amos stood off to the side, messing with a spell phone in his hand.

"Okay, either the tropics have frozen over or the North Pole is gonna melt. I think I've seen everything now," I exclaimed, pointing at our friend.

Nutty rushed over to the curmudgeon and scrambled his way on top of the nearby bar stool. "Where'd you get that from?"

"Huh?" Amos grunted, not looking up from the screen.

Nutty pointed at the piece of technology. "I've never seen you with one of those before. Heard you call them all kinds of things and say some pretty not nice things about those who use them too much."

"If my memory serves me right, I'm pretty sure you said they'd be the downfall of civilization as we know it," Vale teased.

Amos squinted and brought the screen closer to his eyes. "Well, if I could find what I'm looking for, I think I could prove my point."

I held out my hand palm up. "Give it here and tell me what you're trying to find."

My offer snapped my grumpy friend to attention. "Uh, I don't think that's a good idea. You know what, never mind. I'll just give this back to Wyatt." He hid the phone behind his back and changed his tone to something way more chipper, the wrinkles in his face deepening with a frightening attempt at a smile. "Hey, did you manage to figure out what you wanted to sculpt?"

"Okay, what's going on? What's so important that you tried to use a spell phone?" I asked, scrutinizing his odd behavior.

Amos paused for a second with widened eyes before he gave up. His shoulders slumped forward. "You know what, it's better coming from me than if you overheard it from anyone else."

"What is?" Vale shuffled a few steps closer.

He looked back and forth between the two of us, and then thrust the phone out at Vale. "I heard some of the staff talking about it, so I was trying to find a way to access the Winternet on that infernal contraption to see what was going on."

Vale took the spell phone and stepped closer to Amos so he could watch her. "It's right here if you use this browser. What were you trying to look up?"

He hunched over and spoke in a low voice. "The Evergreen Enquirer."

A surprised chuckle burst out of me. "You know, I never would have taken you as one who liked to be in on all the gossip."

"Not most of it. Just the kind that might hurt one of my friends." Amos glanced up at me, sympathy filling his gaze.

My stomach tightened. Whatever he wanted to find, it must have something to do with me. Maybe that would explain how every member of staff we passed seemed obsessed with me. Most of the time, we didn't take anything that paper published seriously because it sounded so made up. But even salacious news usually had its origins in something real to make it sound believable.

Vale found what Amos had been looking for and after a brief moment of reading, she gasped. "Oh my stars, that's not good."

I rushed forward, anxious to find out. "What? What does it say?"

"Give her the phone," Amos commanded. "Better for her to read for herself."

I accepted the piece in my shaking hand and closed my eyes, taking a deep breath to steady myself. When I was ready, I began the torture of reading.

"The title is something. *Cheating Sleigh Maker Not So Charming*. They included a really flattering picture of me and edited Pandora out." I tried to laugh away the absurdity of it all, but the half-hearted chuckle got stuck in my throat.

Swallowing hard, I continued. "Aurora Hart, best known for how she recreated a sleigh for Santa to use to make his deliveries just in time, admitted that she is not the one who makes her sculptures. According to an unnamed source, she can't do anything without help."

"I hate when they use unnamed source," Amos grumbled. "Either someone is a big coward, or it's completely made up."

I cleared my throat to try to keep my voice from wavering. "And then there's the question of her involvement with the sleigh in the first place. When asked about how she helped solve what had happened to the original sleigh, Hart again said that she was not the one who brought the culprit to justice, which calls into question whether she had anything to do with the whole disappearance of the sleigh in the first place, considering the person caught was her former boss. Did she really save the day or did she manage to create a massive opportunity for herself?"

Nutty's tail twitched in agitation. "Whoever wrote this is twisting things all around."

I tried to read more, but with my thundering heart and with tears on the verge of falling, I couldn't see the screen. Handing off the phone to Vale, I sniffed hard and wiped my hand underneath my nose.

My sensitive friend held my hand as she read the next bit. "Hart's thriving ice sculpture business has been touting itself as offering one-of-a-kind creations from the supposed savior of Christmas, but do the customers really get what they're paying for? When we contacted one of them for an interview, the client admitted that what was received was half the size that was originally requested. If what the source says is true, then Miss Hart's business may melt away from such shady dealings."

Anger replaced my devastation. "Who would have said that? I've never had any complaints about my work, and there's only one customer who I ever changed the size of the sculpture for, but that was at her request."

Vale squeezed my hand. "Remember, this is not a reputable news source. They want to make money off their stories."

"And they're doing it this time off my back," I grumbled, sniffing again.

"Do you want me to stop?" Vale asked, getting a little weepy at how the whole thing affected me.

I blew out a long breath. "No, let's just get it over with. Like ripping off a Band Aid."

My friend nodded. "Of course, Miss Hart is no stranger to doing the wrong thing. It is public knowledge that she arrived in Holiday Haven as a condition of her legal probation from being arrested for theft. While those records were expunged after the sleigh incident, the reasons for her presence in the North Pole bring to question her current business and its validity. Could she be fleecing residents once again?

"Oh, that's just low. You know, I wonder if you'd have a libel case against them." Amos stomped his foot in anger.

Taking off my sunglasses, I wiped a hot tear off my cheek. "It's not libel if the information is true."

"They're making you out like you're some criminal mastermind when that's not the case at all." He clucked his tongue in disapproval and glared at a passerby who couldn't stop gawking at me. "Keep it moving," he growled at the young man, jutting his thumb in the opposite direction.

"Oh, they included that grainy picture of you and Wyatt together on the balcony at the Yule Ball." Vale showed me on the small phone screen. "That was such a romantic moment."

I snorted. "I'm guessing that's not how they're going to spin things. Keep going."

My tiny friend scrolled up for more text. "But her cheating may not be contained to just her business. While Miss Hart was busy stealing the heart of bar owner Wyatt Berenger, it seems that one romantic conquest is not enough to satisfy the ravenous sleigh maker."

"Ravenous!" I shouted. "They're making it out like I'm man crazy."

Vale continued. "When asked directly about her dating status, Miss Hart refused to give a straightforward answer. Her only response was to say that she was off the dating market. Whether that means she is in a committed relationship, choosing to be a confirmed spinster, or chasing after multiple partners remains to be seen."

"Now they're throwing darts at the board. Any one of those things could be true," Amos said.

"But people like to believe the worst," I admitted to myself. "Which means they'll think that I'm a serial dater at best and something far, far uglier at worst." I balled up my fists, wishing I could hit the person who dared to write this fiction.

"We're almost to the end, I promise," Vale warned. "While Aurora Hart has been the darling of the media for a while, it is clear that everything that has been reported about her should come into serious question. And perhaps the community we have built here in the North Pole shouldn't hold someone who cheats as blatantly as Miss Hart allegedly has in such high regard."

A long, tense silence followed after my friend finished reading the article.

Amos stepped forward and placed a hand on my shoulder. "Don't forget that those who know and love you won't believe any of that. They'll ball it up, and it'll be tinder for fire in no time." He patted me a couple of times, which was about as close to a hug as I was going to get.

Nutty jumped off the bar stool and scampered over to hug my ankle. "Yeah, yeah, you know we have your back."

Vale hugged me around my waist. "Absolutely. And Amos is right. Those of us who know you won't believe a word of this."

Their immediate outpouring of support tugged at my heart even more, and more tears fell. I hated feeling so attacked, but what could I do?

"What's going on?" Wyatt asked as he approached our group with Clarence close behind.

Vale moved to give him room to take over the hugging. "The Evergreen Enquirer printed a pretty ugly article about Rory."

My boyfriend drew me tight against him and rocked me back and forth. "I'm so sorry."

Wrapped up in his strong arms, I let myself fall apart. I sobbed into his chest until I made a snotty mess on his shirt. He rubbed my back and kept whispering reassuring things to me until the blubbering subsided into whimpering gasps.

"Who wrote the article?" Wyatt asked, his voice a more animalistic growl than before. "I'd like to have a chat with whoever it was."

With the mess of reporters there for Pandora's little press conference, there was no telling what publication or news outlet they'd work for. It could have been any one of them.

My boyfriend's protective nature actually made it easier to stop crying. With several more sniffs, I backed away from him. "You can't go all full bear on somebody just because they wrote something mean about your girlfriend."

Wyatt's eyes flashed with inhuman intensity. "Sure I can."

"No, you can't," Vale reiterated. "Because there's no name on the article."

"Oh, even better. An anonymous coward," Amos spit on the ground.

"It's positively cold-blooded," agreed Clarence in his posh British accent. "And as a vampire, I should know."

Vale raised her hand in the air to get our attention. "I just searched for Rory's name on the

Winternet, and a lot more positive things are there. Merry Mittens has an entire video, and I doubt she has anything negative to say about you."

"I wish they weren't mentioning me at all," I complained. "But Pandora definitely put me on the spot."

I kept going over the main points of the Enquirer's article in my head, trying to figure out why they had twisted my words to come up with any of it.

"Do you want me to take you back home?" Wyatt asked, concern filling his face. "I'm sure you can back out of creating any ice sculptures for the event. Nobody would blame you."

A couple of young women in staff shirts walked by a few feet away from our group. They stared at Wyatt and then glared at me. One of them whispered something to the other that caused them both to giggle with derision. Nutty scurried over until he popped up right in front of them, causing the girls to squeal and run away.

"I don't know what I want to do," I answered with all honesty. "If I don't do anything, then that will make me look bad. If I do contribute with an ice sculpture, I'm not sure anyone will value it. Or will even believe if I did it myself. But I'll admit, I'm not sure how enthusiastic I am about it anymore."

The click of high heels echoed down the stone path, getting louder as Pandora approached. "You poor darling, I've just heard word about that awful article. You must feel absolutely terrible about it."

I held my head a little higher. "Well, who believes what's written in the Evergreen Enquirer?"

The event planner maneuvered in front of Amos to stand next to Wyatt. "What a good perspective to have about it all. Although," she touched my boyfriend's arm, "it is unfortunate what they wrote about your dating situation. I'm surprised that you didn't shout it from the rooftops about being together with this fine man. If he were mine, I'd make sure everybody knew."

"Everybody who matters already does," Amos said from behind her.

Pandora ignored him. "I guess it makes sense that you won't be doing a sculpture for the solstice celebration. Such a shame, but I totally understand if you want to save your reputation by pulling out."

I crossed my arms. "I'm not sure quitting would make me look particularly good. I think it would give more credibility to the article's allegations."

"It's not even an article." Amos pointed at the phone still in Vale's hand. "That's pure gossip."

"And there's lots more coverage in the press that's good. Surely, that outweighs the one bad piece," Vale defended.

Pandora's friendly expression tightened into one more resolute. "But still, any negative press could affect the entire event. You wouldn't want that, would you? You doing the noble thing by pulling out would be very helpful to all those people involved."

"You the most, right?" Something about what she'd said triggered a thought. "Because I recall you mentioning in conversation that you were the one who achieved all of this. And that was in response to me saying I couldn't have done what I do without the help of my friends. Funny how almost those exact same words were twisted in the Enquirer to mean something completely different."

"I'm sure I don't know what you're talking about. But if you insist on following through with an ice sculpture, maybe make it something less noticeable. Maybe place it somewhere...out of the way, m'kay?" She nodded her head once as if her word was the final say.

Wyatt shifted until he stood right beside me. "That's funny. Yesterday, you practically made it impossible for Rory to refuse to make something for your event. And today, after one article in a less-than-reputable source, you suddenly don't want her work featured?"

Pandora clutched her neck, but she wore no pearls today. "Oh, I'm sorry if I gave off the impression that her work isn't wanted. I'm just worried that something might happen to it. It is only ice, and with the temperature in here, I'm a little afraid it might be more vulnerable than usual. That's all."

Her shaky laugh after that statement exposed her own discomfort. A trickle of sweat ran down the side of her temple.

Although my belief in Pandora's involvement with the Enquirer grew with every ticking second, I couldn't prove it. And at this point, I wanted to create a sculpture if for nothing else than showing her up.

"If you're positive, then I'm ready to get to work. I think I've got all the inspiration that I need." I extended my hand.

Pandora looked at it as if I had dirt covering every inch of my skin. She winced as the light source above us brightened and shielded her eyes. "I suppose—"

A nearby speaker buzzed to life. "Boss? Boss? There's a problem."

The planner sighed in relief. "Looks like I'm needed elsewhere."

Refusing to let her wiggle her way out of this, I replaced the sunglasses on my face and stepped closer. "A handshake's good enough, right?"

She squinted to be able to see me, her expression less unsure. "If I must." Her hand moved forward to grasp mine.

The speaker squealed, and the panicked voice shouted. "We really need some help here!"

The second our hands touched, a piercing squeal followed by a loud crack rumbled through the dome, and the light above us dimmed a couple of times.

"Whoa, that's some handshake," Amos snarked.

"What's going on?" Pandora whipped out of my grip, all traces of her attempt to remain pleasant gone.

The light source flickered again before disappearing all together. Darkness engulfed the entire place. I could almost hear my own heart beating in the immediate hush that followed. Until a piercing scream shattered the silence.

Chapter Eight

Pandora used the light function on her spell phone to scurry away to fix the problem. The rest of us Humbugs huddled together, using our phones to see each other.

"What in the world is happening?" Vale asked in a hushed whisper.

"I don't know, but I hope whoever just screamed is okay." I reached out to touch Wyatt to help reassure me.

His hand found mine, and he pulled me closer to him. "I think whatever Pandora's been using to power this whole place just failed."

"If it's one of Pandora's spells, then I guess she can just spellcast it again." Vale shrugged in the pale glow from her spell phone.

"Hmph," Amos grunted, crossing his arms and

tipping back on his heels. "I've never seen a spell go wrong like that, and I've been around for a few years."

"Just a few?" Clarence teased. "That makes you quite young."

The joke earned the vampire a rare chortle from Amos. "If you ask me, that seemed more like a voltage problem. The dimming of that infernal sun above us is like when the current in the transformer isn't running right. Or that a circuit got overloaded."

"I concur with my friend," Clarence agreed. "In fact, I volunteer to take on the role as Sherlock Holmes and investigate."

"But you don't have anything to light your way," countered Vale.

The vampire smiled, and his fangs seemed to gleam all on their own. "I neither need nor require light to see. If you'll pardon me, I must fly."

I blinked, sure someone had played a trick on me. One second, the pub owner stood in front of us and the next, the space he'd occupied was empty.

"I was kind of hoping he'd poof into a bat," Amos complained.

Vale smacked our friend's arm in playful admonishment. "What about that scream? I hope whoever it was is okay."

"Yeah, yeah, maybe they're just scared." Nutty

hugged my ankle, and I picked the nervous guy up and placed him on my shoulder.

Wyatt squeezed my hand and let go. "Well, if we want to try and find out what's going on, we better get moving."

"Um, I think you're forgetting that none of the rest of us are vampires." I gestured around at all the darkness. "The reach of our spell phones will only go so far."

"Vampires aren't the only ones who can see in the dark." He kissed my cheek and undid the button at the top of his shorts. "Just give me a second to finish changing over there."

My cheeks warmed at the thought of Wyatt stripping down to change into his animal. I remembered the first time he'd revealed himself to me and all the other times since, and it never got old.

Familiar huffs and grunts reached my ears, and I turned in the direction of the noises where my boyfriend had gone to change. A shadowed mass lumbered in our direction, its eyes reflecting the light from the spell phones aimed at it. Wyatt's bear approached me with great care and bumped against me. I stumbled a bit, and Nutty lost his perch on my shoulder.

"I'm okay," my roommate confirmed after he hit the sand floor.

The bear chuffed in apology before lowering

himself onto his belly. I gawked at his unusual position.

"Get on," Nutty commanded. "He wants you to ride on his back, and I should know. I speak fluent bear."

Wyatt had let me ride him a few times, but he knew it wasn't my favorite form of transportation since I tended to fall off if he went fast. Still, I didn't see how else I could explore our darkened environment.

I placed my spell phone in my pocket. Grabbing Wyatt's fur around his scruff, I hoisted one leg over the massive bulk of his animal's body. Once I got settled, I patted his head to let him know. With slow deliberation, he stood up and let me gain my balance.

"Can I go, too?" Nutty asked.

Wyatt nodded once, and my roommate climbed the fur and settled himself on top of the bear's head. I almost scolded him for being disrespectful, but the sight of a squirrel petting a bear amused me too much.

"Don't go too fast," I pleaded with Wyatt's animal. "Remember last time." It had taken more than two weeks for the huge bruise on my behind from my last fall to heal.

Wyatt took a few tentative steps forward, his lumbering pace about as fast as a snail's.

I rolled my eyes. "Thanks, but I didn't mean that

slow. At this rate, we'll be here until tomorrow. And since whatever malfunctioned has killed any blowing breezes, I would think you'd want to get a move on since you've got to be hot under all that fur."

Wyatt woofed at me and moved a little faster, but not so brisk that I risked falling off. I couldn't see anything in the dark, but his bear kept moving forward without bumping into anything.

"Pardon me," Clarence called out from the darkness in front of us.

My heart leaped into my throat as he caught us off guard. Wyatt growled a little, his chest vibrating against my legs. Pulling my spell phone out of my pocket, I spotlighted the vampire. His pupils reflected like they were made of mirrors, causing an unearthly glow in them.

"My sincerest apologies for catching you off guard." The pub owner bowed his head once. "But I was on my way back to the group when I caught sight of you coming my way. It seems Amos was right in his assessment. There is a mechanical system running things for the whole dome, but it seems to run on some sort of magic rather than electricity."

"Did Pandora let you get close enough to see it?" I asked.

Clarence frowned. "I did not find the unpleasant woman nor catch a whiff of her scent. Wherever she disappeared to, it was nowhere near that source of the issue. I did overhear two people arguing over whether or not they could get the system working again."

"Sounds a lot like what we heard before," Nutty observed.

I'd forgotten all about our earlier encounter after the discovery of the awful article. "I wonder if it was one of the same people involved. I wish we'd gotten a look at them."

Clarence held up his finger to stop me from talking. "Do you hear that?"

I clamped my mouth shut and listened. "I can hear a few voices, but it sounds like staff wondering what to do."

The vampire shook his head. "It is possible your mortal ears can't detect it. But there is a tête-à-tête that is becoming quite heated in that direction. I believe Pandora is involved."

I adjusted my seat on Wyatt's back. "Can you lead us there?"

Clarence tipped his head to the side. "From the sounds of it, we may not make it in time. If you would like, I could go and observe to report back to you."

"I'd like to hear what dear ol' Pandy has to say about all of this. Based on what Nutty and I heard earlier, the boss of everything may be completely to blame." An idea popped in my head. "Is there any way you could get me there?"

My request caught the vampire by surprise and his typically smooth demeanor faltered. "I...of course, but..." He cleared his throat. "It would be my pleasure, although I would like reassurances from your paramour that he approves. I have no desire to provoke an attack. You have no idea how long it takes to grow an entire limb back."

I scoffed at his joke until Clarence's serious countenance sobered me. Patting Wyatt's head, I asked, "Are you okay with it?"

The bear chuffed and shifted where he stood. Nutty stood up on his head. "He doesn't like it, but he's not saying no."

Wyatt lowered his body to make it easier for me to climb off him. Burying my head against his fur, I gave him a big squeeze. "I'll try not to get into trouble."

Clarence placed his hand over his un-beating heart. "I give you my word I will take good care of her. Begging your pardon, Miss Rory, if you are ready."

I nodded, and by the time I finished, I found myself cradled in the vampire's arms. His cold presence cooled my heated body.

"You may want to loop your arms around my neck

and hold on tight." He waited for me to comply. "I would instruct you to close your eyes because the speed may be disorienting, but with the lack of illumination in here, I do not think you will experience any adverse effects."

Before I could reply, the air around me blew against my face as the vampire transported me using his supernatural speed. He may not have transformed into a bat, but we definitely flew. Despite not being able to see in the dark, I still squeezed my eyes tight.

The force of the wind whipping around us lessened as Clarence slowed. The vampire's mouth leaned closer to my ear. "Stay very quiet and listen." He placed me down with great care and without a grunt of effort.

"You aren't hearing me," Pandora hissed. "This is completely unacceptable."

"But you said to do whatever it takes," a familiar high-pitched voice squeaked in response. "Despite my warnings, we managed to fulfill your request even though it didn't do any good or achieve what you wanted."

The angrier Pandora became, the stronger her accent came out. "My reasons are my own, and I don't pay you to worry about the why's. I pay you to get things done."

"We're working on it, but honestly, this is above our pay grade. You may want to consider getting everyone out of here for their own safety," the high-pitched voice warned.

"That is not an option," the event planner countered. "I already sunk too much time and money, not to mention expending all of that magic to transport some of the specialized staff. I will not send them away just to need them back again. No, until you've exhausted all of your resources, everybody will have to stay here."

"Without the system running, the temperature will change to match the outside environment," her employee explained. "So, anybody in here who is not prepared for the cold may get injured."

"Then they'll have to find a way to stay warm," Pandora dismissed with a callous coolness. "Now, stop trying to tell me how to run my own business and fix things."

"Fine," agreed the high-pitched voice. "But it'll cost you."

"That's utter extortion," the event planner protested.

"Or I could call your friend at that gossip outlet and give them an exclusive story about all of the safety measures you told us to bypass to increase the temperature in here."

"But that's not what happened. You can't just lie like that," Pandora whined.

I dug my fingernails into the palms of my hand to

keep myself from bursting forward and calling her a hypocrite.

A loud buzzing echoed across the dome, and an alarm bell clanged three times. Clarence moved closer to me.

"What was that?" Pandora exclaimed, asking the same question I had.

"Sounds like the system might be recovering after cooling down and about to come back on," her employee said. "But I stand by what I said. If you want things to keep running, then you'll have to pay me more."

"Fine," the planner gritted. "Whatever it takes."

Clarence picked me back up in his arms. "We need to leave now," he whispered into my ear. "Before the light comes back and we are discovered."

He took off before I could protest. As we moved away, the light at the top of the dome flickered on and off a couple of times. The vampire found a safe place to let me down, and once my feet hit the sand, the ball of light at the top blazed back to life.

I blinked hard as my eyes adjusted. Wyatt's bear shuffled over to join us with Nutty still riding on his head.

"Yeah, yeah, so did you figure out what's going on?" my roommate asked.

I opened my mouth to answer but found I didn't have a ready reply. Pandora had some part to play, but what that was hadn't made itself clear yet. We needed to find out who the high-pitched voice belonged to and interrogate that being. And just how dangerous was the system running the temperature inside the dome?

"No," I admitted to Nutty. "We didn't get any clear answers. But we may have discovered another mystery that needs to be solved."

The sound system crackled to life again, and Pandora's voice echoed across the entire space. "Ladies and gentlemen, as you can see, things have returned to normal. I thank you for your patience, but at this time, I would like to ask that any additional guests or non-staff please leave the premises. Thank you," she crooned, as if her previous argument had never happened.

Wyatt rejoined us, buttoning up his shirt. "I think she means us."

"I guess she found a way to get rid of us," I said, not even trying to hide my disappointment. "We'll have to come back tomorrow."

"If she'll even let us in," Vale added. "What are the chances we won't be allowed back in. Although I really shouldn't take another day off. We've got a shipment of dark chocolate coming in tomorrow that I don't want to miss."

My friend had a good point. How could we investigate if we couldn't gain access?

Wyatt massaged my tense neck. "With everything Pandora's dealing with right now, I doubt she'd even be concerned about the list."

I brightened. "True, let's speak to Alfie on the way out."

"And if it helps, I'll allow you to raid Yuletide Yummies before you head out here tomorrow so you can bribe your way in," Vale offered.

I winked at her. "I like the way you think."

Chapter Nine

The bell on the front door of Yuletide Yummies chimed as we stopped by to pick up the promised boxes of goodies to take with us to the event site. Instead of being greeted by Vale's eternally smiling face, she pushed through the swinging door with a frown. She wiped her hands on her dirty apron covered in brown stains.

"What's wrong?" I asked.

"The chocolate shipment. The whole thing is ruined," she complained.

I rushed over to give her a hug despite the threat of staining my own coat. It threw me off to have her be so upset. "How is it ruined? Is there anything salvageable?"

She shook her head. "All of the contents were

completely melted when they arrived. It was one big soupy bittersweet mess."

Wyatt stepped forward. "How did that happen?"

Vale shrugged. "The shipping company said that it had happened in transportation, which they claim is the fault of the supplier. The supplier says it's the fault of the shipping company. So, basically, I'm stuck in the middle without a very important supply for my business."

"Can your dad get something sent to him to tide you over?" I asked. The owner of the Gingerbread General could always get his hands on whatever anyone needed.

Vale busied herself putting some of the baked goods into boxes. "Papa says a lot of his delivery was ruined as well. Mama says he's busy trying to sort things out on his end."

"What will you do?" I asked, worried for my friend.

She drew in a deep breath and attempted a smile. "Stop moping and figure something out. The chocolate debacle really only affects me and my truffles. There's plenty more we can make for the store. Here, I hope this helps you gain entrance today." She handed me the boxes of goodies.

I offered her another hug, but she laughed and pushed me away to avoid getting more chocolate on me. Wyatt and I thanked her and went outside to join Amos. The older man's arms gesticulated wildly, trying to convince our vampire friend to ride with him.

"It's much appreciated, old friend," Clarence said. "But I should stay at the Wassail today." He waved a greeting to us. "I wish you the best and invite you over for a pint when you are finished."

Nutty climbed his way to the front of Amos's snowmobile. "You're gonna let me drive this time, right?"

"Eh, maybe with a little help," Amos said, winking at me. "What did you get all over your coat, Rory?"

I handed off the boxes to Wyatt so I could mount the back of his snowmobile. "I'll tell you later."

A hard breeze blew down the main street, and I prepared to zip my coat up to the very top. Instead of freezing me, it actually felt warm.

"That's odd," I said, glancing up at the gray skies. "The clouds look like they're promising snow."

Wyatt sniffed the air. "Doesn't smell like it. And the temperature is way off."

"Those aren't snow clouds. They're something else," Amos noticed. "But we better get going. I'm not getting any younger or better looking standing here." He started his motor.

Wyatt placed his helmet on his head. "I've got a bad feeling." He handed me the boxes to hold. "I'll drive slow enough so you can hang on with one hand."

Amos and Nutty took the lead, and Wyatt followed along behind them a little slower. When we drove through the open field toward the dome, but we stopped way further out than before.

"Look," Wyatt said, pointing ahead.

The parking area in front of the entrance had no snow covering it. Green and brown patches of grass spread out several yards in front of the beach bubble.

"I think I have a bad feeling, too," I said, getting help off the back of the vehicle.

The four of us walked through the soggy field in our boots. I spotted a snow bunting as it pecked at the ground, hunting for worms. With its snowy white breast and gray-speckled wings, it normally blended into the winter environment. But it stood out against the bare ground.

Alfie left his post to address us as we approached. "Do you guys know what happened yesterday?"

"No, we were going to ask you about it," I said. "When we left, I'm pretty sure there was still standing snow."

The Yeti picked up one of his feet, his white shaggy fur stained with dirt. "When I clocked in this morning, I couldn't believe the condition of the area. I asked my colleague about it, and he told me we were only paid to make sure the right people come inside." He eyed the box of goodies I carried.

I opened it up for him to choose what he wanted. "Are we still on the list?"

Alfie stuffed a gingerbread man into his mouth and bit it in half. "We were told nobody else was to go in or out today." He finished the rest of the cookie in one more bite.

I offered him more from the box. "Any chance there's another way inside?"

The Yeti glanced over at his colleague who was busy with his phone. Alfie beckoned for us to follow him and walked us around the dome until we were out of sight. He rapped his knuckle against the surface of the bubble and leaned his head in to listen.

"What are you doing?" Amos asked.

"Per safety regulations, there has to be an exit here somewhere. Miss Ashmore spared no expense to make sure it was camouflaged to keep others from finding it and ruining her beautiful illusion." His bushy eyebrows knitted together, and he took a step back, knocking on the structure again. "I think I've found it."

Our friend tapped his knuckles around the area until he was satisfied. "If I push here..." He leaned his body against the edifice, and a door opened inwardly.

"Has anyone ever told you you're brilliant?" I said, handing him both boxes. "If I were you, I'd eat everything and leave your partner nothing. Not even the crumbs."

He pulled a sticky bear claw out of the box and chewed on it. "To be honest, I'm tired of this job. If this ends up getting me fired, then so be it. I'm only staying to try and find out what in the world is going on. If letting you guys get inside helps with that, then it's worth losing my position."

"Aw, Alfie, I hope that doesn't happen. If we don't see you at the day's end, come join us at the Whet Your Wassail pub and we'll fill you in." I almost offered a hand to shake but decided against it as the Yeti licked off the sticky sugar from his fingers. Patting him on his large arm, I led the charge inside.

With only a couple of days left to prepare, we expected to find the staff in total chaos. What we found when we fully entered the premise shocked us.

"Nobody's rushing around or panicking," I observed, peeling off my coat.

Amos set Nutty down and followed suit. "And the air is still pretty hot. With hardly any breeze blowing."

"After what Clarence and I heard, I would imagine the system would be at risk again if it gets too hot." I remembered my desire to identify who the high-pitched voice belonged to.

Wyatt took my coat and stashed it behind a hibiscus plant. I licked the little bit of chocolate from my hug with Vale this morning and stopped mid lap. "The snow is melted," I noticed.

"Yeah, we already established that," Amos groused.

I shook my head. "No, you don't get it. The snow was melted much further away from the bubble. And Vale's shipment of dark chocolate came in completely melted and ruined."

Wyatt caught onto my train of thought. "That must mean that something is affecting the transportation in and out of Holiday Haven. And whatever that is, maybe it starts from right here."

"And if that's the case, then Pandora's got more of a problem on her hands than a messed-up solstice celebration." A sobering idea occurred to me. "What if this predicament spreads even further. Like, what happens if the melting extends all the way into town? Or into all of the North Pole?"

"Shh." Wyatt kissed the top of my head. "Let's tackle one obstacle at a time. You may be right, but if there's any more drastic changes in the environment, there are probably measures to help from the big guy."

I whipped out my spell phone. "I could always call on Clara."

My finger hovered over my friend's name. While she had stayed in my life and even frequented the

Break Room on occasion, I didn't want to abuse my friendship with such a huge celebrity.

"Why don't we try and see what we can find out first so that if you do need to call her, you have specifics rather than speculations," Wyatt suggested, clapping his hands together. "With that in mind, what's the plan?"

Amos scratched his chin stubble. "I'd like to find whatever's running the environment in this place and see if I can figure it out."

Nutty stuck his little paw in the air. "I'm gonna question some of the invisible inhabitants in here."

I tilted my head in interest. "Like who?"

"Maybe one of those red things that was crawling on the edge of the water. It had these snapping things for hands, and it moved sideways like this." Nutty's paws opened and closed as he scooted from side to side.

"You mean a crab?" I giggled.

"Yeah, yeah, one of those," he exclaimed with excitement. "When you're little like me, everybody ignores you. But we're usually the ones who see everything."

I pulled out a surprise from my pocket. "I was saving this for later, but I think you deserve it now. I rescued it from one of Vale's brownies." I held out a large pecan in front of my roommate.

The squirrel's tail twitched with delight, and he

snatched the nut from me. "This is why you're the best roomie ever! I hope we're always together forever and ever."

I didn't have the heart to tell my little buddy that ever since Wyatt had invited me to stay with him, I'd been considering alternative possibilities for my living situation. That kind of information needed to wait for a more private moment. Or until I could get my hands on a large stash of nuts to help ease the pain.

"I'd like to find Barnacle Bill again and see if he could clarify things for me as to who's really in charge of this whole thing," I said, thinking about the kind pelican. "And maybe try to find Mistletoe. I haven't seen her since our first day here."

One of the young men I recognized as working with Wyatt at the tiki bar the day prior caught sight of us and changed directions to come intercept us. He waved his hand at my boyfriend.

"Mr. Berenger, I'm so glad you're here. Somebody told me that you wouldn't be joining us today, and we really need your help," he said with breathless relief.

"Hey, Eric," Wyatt greeted him. "What seems to be the problem?"

"We've lost the main ingredient for almost all of your drink specials, and none of us know what to do without it."

Wyatt furrowed his brow. "What's missing?"

The young man's eyes widened. "That stuff you called Santa's snow. Tyler swears he put it in the refrigerator before things shut down last night, but when we went to get it out to help practice making the drinks one more time, the whole metal container was just...gone."

"Things don't just up and walk away on their own. Let me see if I can help you out. Just give me five more minutes." Wyatt held up his hand to indicate how long he needed.

Eric blew out a long breath. "Thanks so much, Mr. Berenger."

"Not a problem. And call me Wyatt," he called after the bartender. "Geez, all these kids are making me feel ancient. I keep wanting to turn around to find my father when they call me Mr. Berenger. And that's not a man I really want to see."

Wyatt had told me a lot about several of his family members, but he never talked about his father. And the few times he mentioned him, none of the details indicated that he had a very good relationship with him.

I rubbed his arm. "You go help them out. I'm going to talk to a few people and see what I can find out."

"What do we do if we run into Panda and she tells us to leave?" Amos asked, intentionally getting the planner's nickname wrong again.

Our older friend made a good point. I didn't think the event planner would appreciate us breaking into her place, even if it was to try and help her fix a situation, she seemed unwilling to take care of herself.

I took a cue from the blackmailer from the day before. "Try telling her that you'd be happy to get in touch with the Enquirer and tell them all the dirty details about how this whole event is becoming a disaster."

Amos's gray eyebrows raised into his nonexistent hairline. "I have to say, I never expected to hear you get so ruthless. Color me impressed."

"With what she overheard about Pandora's involvement with the article, that woman would deserve it," Wyatt defended. "I don't care if she's a fellow Southerner, I'm ready to bless her heart and knock her sideways next time I lay eyes on her.

I chuckled. "You know, your accent gets stronger when you're agitated." I didn't add that Pandora's did, too. No point in poking an angry bear when he's riled up. "Besides, you're gonna have to get in line after me."

Amos chortled with glee. "I don't know if I've become a bad influence on the two of you or if you're finally growing up. Either way, petty looks good on the both of you." He took off to explore the perimeter of the dome, still chuckling.

Wyatt pulled me in for a big hug. "Sorry, I get overly protective. I know you can take care of yourself. But I'm never going to like it when someone hurts you, and my bear will tear me from the inside out if I can't look after you."

I snuggled in a little closer and breathed in his familiar, delicious scent. "You and Bear do a fine job. And it makes me feel treasured to have you on my side. But I mean it. I get first crack at Pandora once we figure out what's going on and why things are melting."

With nobody watching us, he cupped my cheek in his hand and bent down to kiss me. For a wondrous moment, the heat warming my body didn't come from the environment in the dome. We lingered together until we came close to crossing the inappropriate line.

Wyatt pulled away first, his eyes shining bright. "You know, you're pretty amazing."

"Back atcha, big guy." I tried taking a step forward but stumbled a bit, still a little punch drunk from the kiss.

Wyatt's smile turned a little cocky from his effect on me. "I'll come find you when I'm finished."

"How will you know where I am?" I asked.

"Because I'll always know where you are." He tapped his nose. "Plus, when in doubt, I can follow your scent."

I pulled my T-shirt away from my body and sniffed it. "Do I stink?"

Wyatt led out an audible laugh and took some backward steps away from me. "No, but your scent is imprinted in me. Face it, Aurora Hart. I intend to make you mine forever and ever."

I called after him. "That's a long time. How about we just get through today first?"

"Deal!" He wiggled his fingers at me before turning around and heading to help at the bar.

"Crazy man," I muttered under my breath before finding the stone path and the first trail marker with the signs pointing in the direction of the shops.

I needed to find a pirate of a pelican to find some answers.

Chapter Ten

U nlike the previous day when the staff had
time to gawk and make fun of me because
of the gossip article from the Enquirer,
not even one person glanced up from their work or
even took notice as I walked around. I expected at
least someone to be worried about what was a clear
problem from the heat inside to the melted snow on
the outside. But everyone acted as if everything was
normal, and they were only two days away from the
opening of the big event.

More huts were set up than the first time I'd
helped Barnacle Bill. For all my concern over
Pandora, she really had managed to put together
something that would appeal to everyone in town of
all ages. There were a few arcade areas where you

could play games to earn prizes as well as more shops with fun beach-themed knickknacks and attire.

My favorite stall had two young women sorting out different tropical flowers of bright colors so they could put them together to make beautiful leis to sell. Next to that shop was one that featured ukuleles of all different sizes from very tiny to almost the size of a guitar. Several of them were colored, but I couldn't help admiring the glossy wood of one like Makai had when we first met. On the bridge of the instrument was a shiny inlaid flower like those the ladies were using to make leis.

There were so many special things and people who would make the event a success, if I could do anything to help, I would. I just hoped that things wouldn't get worse or that Amos could maybe figure out how the temperature was being controlled so we could stop the melting problem before it got worse.

I reached Barnacle Bill's Bounty shop and leaned over the counter. "Ahoy, there, matey. Anybody here?"

The pelican's head popped up from down below. "Oh, it's you again. I'm glad to see you. Maybe you can help me decide which of these temporary tattoos to apply for the opening day. The turtle, the shark, or the dolphin?" He fanned all the choices out in front of me.

I tapped on the turtle. "This reminds me of the

honu that Makai introduced me to down at the beach. Koa. I like this one the best."

"Sea turtle it is!" Bill exclaimed, putting the others back in their display. "So, now that you've helped me, is there anything I can do for you?"

The pelican's pleasant mood would help make the interrogation go easier. I put on my brightest smile. "Actually, I wanted to ask you a question."

"Fire ye cannons!" he shouted. "Sorry, I'm practicing my pirate speech. It means, go ahead."

I leaned my arms on the counter and tilted closer. "The other day, you said there was a boss in charge and then there was the real person in charge. I need to know what that means."

Bill's mood changed in an instant. "You know what, I think I have some stock in the back. I'm not interested in choosing sides. While I might be playing a pirate, I'm really not the cutthroat type."

"Wait, wait," I called out to him. "I don't mean to put you in a bad position or for you to have to choose sides. I'm trying to understand which sides are which. And to figure out who is really in charge. Especially after what happened yesterday."

The pelican pulled the stepladder over and climbed up it so he could get closer to my eye level. "Were you here for the blackout? That was really scary."

"It was really strange. And today, it's even hotter

than ever." I wiped the sweat off my brow for emphasis. "Have you even seen what's happened outside?"

"Oh, no. Those of us who were transported here for this event aren't allowed to leave. It would be pretty funny for me or one of the mermaids to try to go outside into the freezing cold. Only the locals of the North Pole come and go," he explained.

"But that's just it. The warmth from inside seems to be leaking. Outside, the snow has completely melted in a pretty wide radius around the whole beach bubble." I pointed toward the front entrance.

Bill's mood soured. "That's not good. Several of us were commenting that the rise in heat was getting uncomfortable, but not completely unbearable. And yet, I heard a couple of my bunk mates saying that they were getting paid under the table to try and make it as warm as possible without breaking things again last night."

"Did you hear who told them to do that?" I pushed.

The pelican shook his head back and forth, the wattle under his beak wobbling. "No, but that's what I mean by not wanting to choose sides. Things were so much better when there was a clear line of who was the captain of this ship. But now, some say it's Miss Ashmore and others say it's the smaller one."

"Does the smaller one have a high-pitched voice?"

I asked with great interest. "Maybe even a bit squeaky?"

"I don't know. I signed a contract with Miss Ashmore's company, so as far as I'm concerned, she's the one who can hire or fire me." Bill clacked his beak to end his point.

I risked upsetting him with one final question. "But are there others who follow someone else's directions?"

Bill rose one more step up his ladder and leaned out over the edge of his hut, looking left and right. Satisfied no one else could hear us, he waved me closer with his wing.

"Don't tell anyone I told you, but yes. Not for all the shops and stuff near here. That's all been run by Miss Ashmore. But she was not the one who made the bigger arrangements," he explained in a low voice.

"Like what?" I asked with a little too much enthusiasm.

The pelican shushed me and paused to make sure I hadn't garnered any unwanted attention. Taking a deep breath, he answered in a low tone, "Like transporting those of us who aren't locals. Creating the actual structure of the place."

"And controlling the temperature?" I added.

Bill flapped a wing over my mouth. "We're not supposed to talk about that. Whatever's going on with the system, it's all taken care of, according to

Miss Ashmore. And anyone who does talk about it gives her grounds for immediate dismissal."

Nutty appeared on the top of the counter, and the pelican squawked in surprise, almost falling off his step ladder. I introduced him to my roommate, and the bird calmed down a little.

The squirrel jumped up and down. "I helped find the problem."

"You did?" I patted his head in approval. "How'd you do that?"

He stood on his hind legs to his full height, moving his hands to illustrate his tale of detection. "You see, first I found a crab, who told me about the meeting that was had right after he arrived about how everybody was to work in their own sections and to never go near the edge of the bubble. Then I talked to a seagull, who told me all about seeing a lot of commotion in one particular area right by the edge while he was flying around. And then I found this hard gray thing that looked like a weird nut at the edge of the water. It was shaped like this."

The squirrel put his two paws together to show me, and I made my best guess. "You mean an oyster?"

Nutty shrugged. "I guess. I knocked on the hard outside, but it wouldn't open, so I tossed it back into the ocean. But then I thought I'd better tell Amos, so I went to find him, and then the two of us went to inspect the area where the crab was told not to go.

And then Amos sent me to find you. Now, I'm here and you're all caught up."

"What did the two of you find?" I asked.

"I don't know," Nutty admitted. "But Amos thinks he's found a really big problem."

I gave my furry friend my full attention. "Does it have to do with the system controlling the temperature?"

Bill waved his wings at me. "You need to go."

Realizing what a tough position I'd put my new friend in, I apologized. "Thank you for talking to me. I promise you, we're only trying to help. I'm worried that everyone in here is in bigger trouble. Telling you that things are fine and pretending that they are isn't going to fix the problem."

The pelican tilted his head in thought. "Then I hope I gave you something to work with. But please be careful."

I promised him I would and headed off with Nutty bounding across the floor in front of me. My heart raced in anticipation of setting eyes on whatever it was that affected the environment of the beach bubble. However, when we met up with Amos at the far edge of the structure, I couldn't see anything other than the almost transparent side of the dome and a small flowerpot with a tropical plant wilting inside it.

"Where's the mechanism?" I asked.

Amos pointed at the plant. "That's part of it."

I touched the sagging leaf. "All I see is greenery that's in dire need of water."

"No, not the plant itself. What's hidden inside the pot." He crouched down and pulled the neglected frond to the side with great care. "See?"

I knelt on the dirty floor and took a closer look. Shiny rocks were placed in a circle around the perimeter of the pot with some crystal towers sitting in the center. "What are they?"

"I think they're a major part of what was creating the entire atmosphere. From what I can identify, those stones all work with fire and air energies." He pointed at them.

I reached in to pick one up to examine it, and he slapped me hard enough to make my skin sting. "Ow, what did you do that for?"

"They're laid out in a very specific formation, and if you move one, there's no telling how that will affect things." He directed my attention to the crystal in the center. "See how brown it is?"

Kneeling forward, I got as close as he would let me. "It looks almost like its rotten. Or that it might just crumble. What kind of crystal is that?"

"Well, I think it's what's left of a crystal cluster of citrine, which can be used to help focus fire energy." Amos dug in his pocket and pulled out a yellow-orange shard. "I found this half buried in the sand a few yards down that way."

He handed me the broken piece so I could inspect it. The second it touched my palm, it warmed up considerably. The hint of its energy spoke to my own magic.

"There are pots like this lining the entire perimeter, camouflaged by the plants," he explained.

"Helping to create the beautiful illusion," I added.

"Exactly." Amos asked for the citrine shard back. He held it between his thumb and forefinger. "But that's all this is. An illusion that is about to shatter, and when it does, everyone inside and out is going to suffer the consequences."

I gawked at him. "How bad is it?"

"I found this crystal shard right over there. But when I went to trace where it came from, I found pieces of broken terra-cotta. Like this." He tapped the side of the pot. "Remember that weird sound we heard last night before the whole place went dark?"

"Yeah, it was right when I was shaking Pandora's hand." I remembered she was shaking like a leaf in that moment, which I thought at the time indicated how I'd gotten the upper hand.

"This fragment of citrine came off one much bigger. And the one in this pot here is almost to its breaking point, although it looks like whatever energy it was conducting has used it up almost completely." The older man scratched his bald pate.

"Which means whatever magical powers it was helping with will be weakened at this spot," I guessed, hoping not to be right.

Amos nodded and dug in his pocket again and pulled out a large piece of orange-colored pottery. "Based on this, and other shrapnel I discovered, I think there are smaller pots and then some much larger ones placed in strategic spots. This belonged to something bigger than the one sitting here." He tapped the pot in front of us with his broken piece. "I think whatever the crystals were channeling, it got out of hand. And the whole thing exploded."

"Yeah, yeah," Nutty agreed, crawling around the smaller pot with excitement. "I helped find some of the smaller pieces, too. Whatever it was went boom! And then whoosh. Darkness."

I swallowed hard. "Explosions and big booms are not what you want to hear about when you're standing in a magical dome that seems like it's pretty fragile."

Amos snorted. "If that makes you uncomfortable, then you better hold onto your britches." He stood and walked over to the very edge of the bubble. "I know your fire and ice magic kind of works because you create ice and then melt it afterwards. But do you know what happens if you were to heat up a glass bowl until it was piping hot and then plunged it into ice cold water?"

I raised my eyebrows in alarm. "I'm guessing nothing good."

"It goes through thermal shock. And shatters." He waved me over to join him.

A big part of me didn't want to know why Amos had asked me the question. I took a closer look at the wrinkle in the dome that his finger traced.

"That's why I had Nutty come get you. This is one of five I've already found," he said. "And if I walked the entire rim of this place, I'm pretty sure I'd find more."

"What is it?" I asked.

"This big bubble is being heated on the inside. And I'm guessing all that warmth was being contained with magic for a little while, but as time's gone on, that magic's been failing." Amos frowned. "Which is why the snow's melted on the outside."

"So, the heat's definitely leaking out like I thought." Hugging my arms around my body offered very little comfort.

Proving my suspicions were true didn't bring me any satisfaction. Instead, a new form of panic took hold. "If what we think is true, then we don't have any time to waste. I'm guessing this dome will burst like a heated glass bowl being doused in ice cold water."

Nutty nodded his furry head. "Big boom."

"This whole place could fracture in one spectacular disaster." Amos ran his hand down the warped surface of the structure. "We need to find Pandora right now."

"That's going to be a problem," Mistletoe said from right behind me, causing me to jump.

Amos grimaced at the floating fairy. "Why?"

Mistletoe's wings quivered. "Because she's disappeared."

Chapter Eleven

"What do you mean Pandora's gone?" I asked after the fairy assistant's words sunk in. "Where did she go? Are you aware of the melting issue outside?" I pressed.

Mistletoe bobbed up and down in agitation, her wings flitting and shedding more of her pale pink dust. "I am. But when she arrived this morning, she acted like nothing was wrong. I told her that I scheduled a call with the ELF, but before I could brief her, I got called away. By the time I was done, she was nowhere to be seen."

"Who's this elf?" I asked.

"Not a who but a what," the fairy clarified. "ELF stands for the North Pole's Environment & Life Foundation. Since whatever's happening on the inside of the bubble seems to be affecting the outside, I thought it prudent for Pandora to connect with them to get some advice before things get worse."

I furrowed my brow. "Asking for help doesn't sound like something Pandora would do, but I definitely think we could use some help. I'm glad to hear that she's doing something."

Mistletoe dropped a few inches, her face crumpling into a frown. "That's the problem. She was supposed to talk to the ELF. But their representative called me back and said that they never heard from Pandora." The fairy turned this way and that in the air. "Nobody has seen or heard from her since this morning, and there are more fires that need putting out."

"Like the fact that the entire system you're using to heat the inside is failing?" Amos stepped forward and held out his hand. The broken piece of citrine glistened orange in his palm.

The fairy assistant's wings drooped. "So, you know the bigger problem on hand."

"I know that whatever magic that's been keeping the whole shebang running ain't gonna work for very much longer. The person who put the whole spell together needs to rework things and fast, so finding Panda needs to become your number one priority," he insisted.

I watched the fairy with great care, noticing a

change in her expression. "I'm not sure Pandora's the one we need to find."

Amos scoffed. "And why not? It's her mess we're trying to help clean up."

Mistletoe's eyes flitted to me, and the alarm in them gave me the answer to a question I'd already asked Barnacle Bill. "Because I don't think Pandora's really the one who's been running things. It's you, isn't it?"

The fairy assistant bobbed up and down in admission. "How did you know?"

"It occurred to me that Pandora's an awful lot of show and talk, but while she's doing the talking and garnering all the attention, everything else is getting done. That can't happen unless she had someone running things behind the scenes." Another thought occurred to me. "And I think you're probably much more powerful than anyone gives you credit for. Like with your amazing glamour abilities on my first day here."

Nutty's tail twitched in amusement. "You're the reason why Rory looked so pretty in the pictures?"

The fairy's entire demeanor shifted, and her wings lifted to their full height with pride. "Did I help?"

"Oh, absolutely. I mean, I got into my own trouble with some of the answers I gave the reporters, but at least I looked my absolute best," I gushed. "And to be honest, the glamour didn't wear off for almost the rest of the day. I'm sure it annoyed Pandora down to her very sweet, Southern core."

That little tidbit elated the fairy. She vibrated with happiness, causing more fairy dust to fall from her wings. "Well, what she was trying to do, ambushing you with the press, was out of order. I hope you've managed to keep her away from your boyfriend. When she sets her sights on something she wants, she's pretty ruthless in obtaining it." Mistletoe added something under her breath, and I could have sworn I heard her say, "I should know."

Amos cleared his throat. "Now that we've established that we may not need Pandora right this moment, can we get down to what really matters? What are you going to do about this?" He held up the broken citrine crystal in front of her.

"I did my best to get a replacement for the one that cracked last night," she said. "I thought that fixed everything, but then you saw what was happening outside."

Amos beckoned her to inspect the nearby pot. "But you don't need just one replacement. I think you're going to need a whole bunch of them." He showed her the stones in the pot.

Mistletoe frowned as she touched the tip of the spent citrine crystal in the middle. "This shouldn't be happening. At least, not the way I set everything up. All the stones and crystals should be working in harmony to create a pleasant environment inside. Nothing that the beach bubble couldn't contain."

"Except you know that isn't what's happening," Amos replied with impatience. "And I've only inspected a couple of the pots around the edges. No telling what condition they're all in."

"But it doesn't make sense. I was very careful in how each stone was laid out, alternating fire and air elements in a specific pattern." Mistletoe stroked the ailing citrine with her fingers. "I can at least get this one replaced right now."

With a flourish of her hand, her wand appeared in her grasp again. She shook it in front of her and tapped on the wood of the instrument twice until the speakers overhead crackled to life.

"Attention please. Will Shrub please report to me at the northeast designation immediately?" The fairy repeated herself once more and then turned off the PA system with another flick of her wrist.

Amos showed the fairy the wrinkles he'd found earlier and was in the midst of discussing their implications when a minuscule figure walked in our direction. By the style of his clothing, I guessed this was the person Mistletoe had beckoned over the PA.

His pointy leathery ears stood out from under a brown cap, and he wore a pair of drab brown overalls but no shoes to cover his large feet. The toolbox he carried seemed too big for him to handle it, but he moved without struggling.

When he reached us, he let his toolbox drop with a loud crunch. "You called for me?" Shrub asked in a brusque tone. The pitch of his voice caught my attention.

"Yes, we need a new citrine cluster for this pot here. And then you need to get the maintenance team to inspect each of the pots and their contents. Do you have any with you?" Mistletoe asked as she hovered over the crystal that had turned brown.

Shrub exhaled with impatience. "You know, my source for these had to rush our latest order." He pulled off his cap and inspected it as if looking for a flaw in the fabric. "I'm not sure how many stones and crystals we have left at our disposal after the last day."

The fairy furrowed her brow. "That can't be right. I made sure we had plenty just in case something happened."

Amos pulled me aside. "I can't believe they hired him to be in charge of this operation."

"Why not?" I whispered back.

"Because, if I'm not mistaken, he's a gremlin. They aren't known for being the kindest to machinery in any form," my friend explained.

The creature narrowed his eyes at Amos but continued to push about supplies. "I'm sure I can get more of what you want. But my source will require a lot more money in exchange. But maybe if you gave the amount to me in cash, I could speed up the delivery."

The second the gremlin attempted to extort money out of the fairy, I knew without a doubt he must be the same one I'd heard from before. "And let me guess, you'd be pocketing that money?" I accused him.

Shrub scowled at me. "Who are you to accuse me like this?" he growled.

I placed my hand on my hip. "I'm the one who heard you talking to Pandora last night when everything went dark. If I recall, you also asked for money to fulfill her request to get everything working again. Blackmailed her, in fact."

The gremlin glared at me with contempt. "You have proof of this?"

"I wasn't the only one who heard the conversation," I replied with force. "And I'm sure Pandora can attest to it as well if we ask her."

"If you can find her." Shrub's mouth spread into a devious smirk. "Heard the boss ran away. And since the *real* boss is gone, then I guess I don't need to be working at all." He picked up his toolbox and turned to leave.

"You're not going anywhere." Mistletoe waved her

wand at the gremlin, and his feet lifted an inch off the ground.

Shrub struggled to break the magic holding him, and he floundered as he hovered to no avail. The fairy stared at him in disappointment.

"Nutty, do you recall hearing his conversation with another worker the other night?" I asked my roommate.

"Yeah, yeah. Didn't he give that person something to use after he ordered them to 'make it happen.'" The squirrel's impression of the gremlin's demand would almost be humorous if we weren't in such a tough predicament.

Mistletoe kept Shrub contained but paid attention to us. "What was he trying to accomplish?"

"To bury something at the base of whatever was running the magic." I crouched down next to the pot. "Do you think he meant underneath the planter?"

The fairy floated closer to me to look inside. "No, the pot itself isn't acting as the conduit for the magic. The citrine is."

"So, there's something buried underneath the citrine clusters that's messing with the energy flow," Amos clarified. He started to bury his fingers in the soil, but Mistletoe stopped him.

"We don't know what will happen to the citrine if you touch it. I should be the one, but—"

"You need someone to watch Shrub," Amos finished.

Nutty danced from foot to foot in front of the floating gremlin. "I won't let him get away."

Mistletoe smiled at the squirrel's promise. She kept her wand pointed at Shrub but wiggled her fingers at the ground. A small vine sprouted and wrapped itself around the gremlin's legs. Pulling him down from the air, the vegetation continued to bind itself around the unpleasant creature.

With great concentration, the fairy focused on the contents of the pot. She flourished the wand above the soil in a stirring motion. The surface rippled with movement, and several small stones of various colors pushed their way to the top.

"Rory, can you hold out your hands and summon a little of your fire powers into them?" Mistletoe asked.

Puzzled, I did as she asked. The fairy used her magic to lift them from their secret hiding place and moved them into my hands. Each of the smooth rocks felt hot to the touch, and I understood why she wanted me to protect my skin with my own powers.

"I'm guessing these stones conduct fire energies," I observed, fascinated by their interaction with my own magic.

"There's a mix of carnelian, fire opal, and sunstone in there," she confirmed. "They would have boosted the fire element of the configurations to the point where everything would be off balance."

"And that's why it got so hot in here," Amos deduced. "Because your environmental system was thrown off. But why?"

The gremlin stopped struggling against the tightening vines as soon as he realized our collective attention rested on him. Shrub scoffed. "Don't look at me. Unless one of you wants to pay me for the answers, I'm not saying another word."

For one evil moment, I thought about dropping one of the stones still burning in my hands down his overalls, but we didn't need torture him to learn the truth. Now that we knew the reason for the problems, we needed solutions more than confessions.

"Maybe you can dig up all of the fire stones that are affecting the system and that will at least slow things down," Amos suggested. "Give you a chance to make adjustments or find a better solution."

"That's a good place to start," Mistletoe agreed. "But if there are more citrine crystals that need replacing, I'll have to acquire them as soon as possible."

"I can get ahold of Jingle Sugarplum and see if he can help. He's pretty brilliant at procuring goods," I offered.

Mistletoe flicked her wand twice and tapped on it

once to access the sound system again. "Could security please come meet me at the back of the northwest quadrant."

The more I watched the fairy take charge, the more I wondered how much involvement Pandora had in the first place. Since Nutty promised to continue to watch the detained gremlin, Amos, Mistletoe, and I moved to another nearby pot to check its contents.

"I don't know if this isn't the right time to ask this question, but how did Pandora become the face of this event?" I asked the assistant. "Based on what I'm witnessing, you're the foundations of the whole works."

Mistletoe's cheeks flushed a deeper pink than the shade of her wings. "It kind of happened by accident. The whole thing started out by me volunteering to plan some parties for my friends in Garland Gale. And when those went well, I got some offers for payment to plan other events from their friends."

I held up my hand. "Stop. Hold on. Are you saying that the party planning business started off as yours? If that's the case, then how in the world did Pandora end up in charge?"

The fairy used her powers to unearth more of the buried fire stones. Luckily, the citrine cluster in this pot seemed unaffected. "It happened so gradually that I almost didn't notice. When she moved to

Garland Gale, she became the immediate darling with her 'oh, honey' this and 'sweetie' that. She attended one of my events, and afterwards, she approached me and asked if I needed an assistant to help. The business had picked up enough, I could definitely use her help, so I hired her."

"As your assistant? That's a far cry from giving interviews with the press," I said, holding on to the extra stones until they cooled off.

"I never liked the spotlight," Mistletoe explained. "I liked being the person behind the scenes making sure everything happened like clockwork and making the clients happy. So, Pandora volunteered to handle all the press. And little by little, she gained notoriety for being the voice of my business until she became the face of it as well. I should have put a stop to it, but we were getting more work because of how much social buzz she created. Until one day, she started taking credit for my efforts."

"Like she did with her little press conference." Having been manipulated by Pandora at her little ambush, I could see how she outmaneuvered the fairy with the business.

"Exactly. And at first, she had me convinced that it was good for the business for her to be seen as the one responsible for everything. But then, she made it impossible for me to expose the truth." Mistletoe frowned, and her wings fluttered in agitation. "She set me up."

"How?" I asked, not surprised anymore.

"She must have sensed that I was tired of her taking charge, so she created a scenario where while I was helping to clean up after one of the events, I found an envelope full of money." Mistletoe gazed off into the distance as her memories took hold. "I, of course, picked it up and took it back to the office rather than leaving it there with the intent to give it back to the client the next day. Except, the next day, the envelope was gone. And then Pandora showed me the video she had taken of me picking it up in the first place. With her good relationship with the press, she threatened to turn that video in unless I signed the business over to her in full."

"But she couldn't get rid of you altogether because you provided the key ingredient for every event—your magic," I finished for the fairy. "And now that this one is starting to unravel, she's leaving you to take the fall for it all."

Mistletoe shook her head. "I can't be worried about that now. It's more important that we stop the damage that's already happened."

A Yeti approached us, and I sighed in relief until I realized it wasn't Alfie. However, the sight of Topper, Holiday Haven's one law enforcement representative, concerned me more and brought back a few unwanted memories of our last legal encounter.

"What's going on?" I asked the man in uniform.

He looped his hands through his belt. "There are ELF representatives outside with some other official looking folks. Says they have an order for this whole shebang to stop."

"What does that mean?" Mistletoe asked.

Topper twitched his gray mustache. "I'm afraid it means this whole place is getting shut down."

Chapter Twelve

Mistletoe unwound the vines holding Shrub and asked the Yeti guard to watch over him. Instead of cowering in front of the large, hairy sentinel, the gremlin smirked with a little too much smugness. When Shrub caught me looking at him, he drained all emotions from his face.

A female elf with long dark hair and dressed in full winter gear joined us. The longer she stayed inside, the more uncomfortable she became. She played with the zipper on her jacket that had the letters E.L.F. embroidered on it but never took it off, choosing to withstand the heat for as long as possible.

She took out a piece of paper from a folder and placed some reading glasses on the end of her nose.

Clearing her throat, she read the contents out loud. "It has come to our attention that an unnatural phenomenon has created an environmental threat in the Holiday Haven region. Until all investigations have been completed, all work must halt immediately. All persons involved must vacate the premises with rapid haste." She folded the declaration again and took off her glasses, brushing her dark hair over her shoulder.

Several of the employees who had caught whiff of something going on gathered around us. Murmurs of curiosity and anxious nerves rose among the growing crowd.

"An evacuation might be a good idea, but you should know that there are some folks in here who can't just leave," I said, thinking about Makai and Kailani. "As guests brought in specifically for the event, they aren't suited for the colder weather outside."

That information took the elf by surprise, and her professional demeanor faltered a bit. "Appropriate accommodations should always be provided for any hired assistance as well as the necessary paperwork filed. I have checked your town's permits and have found no evidence of unacceptable staff."

I turned to face Mistletoe. "Let me guess. Pandora told you everything had been taken care of."

"She did. And honestly, she's usually good about

getting the paperwork taken care of," the fairy admitted. "I had so many other things to work on, I didn't question whether or not she had done things the right way."

"Those guests should be sent back to wherever they came from right away," the ELF representative commanded.

Topper spoke up in his slow manner. "Well, that there might be a problem. You see, we've had to put a stop to anything being transported in or out of Holiday Haven for the moment unless it's items being brought here locally."

The exasperated dark-haired elf lost a little of her cool. "Sweet Santa, why?"

The officer shuffled from foot to foot. "You see, there were some problems with the shipments that arrived this morning, and based on the evidence I found when investigating, I felt it prudent to put a hold on things until we found a solution."

"Surely things are not so bad that we can't just open the transport channels to send a few people back to where they came from," the elf countered.

"After seeing the aftermath of a shipment of dark chocolate turned into an ooey gooey melted mess, I'm not so sure you want to take that chance," I warned.

The ELF representative pinched the bridge of her

nose. "This is way above my position. I need to contact my superior and find out what steps to take next. In the meantime, you need to get everybody to evacuate those who are available to leave. That includes all of you."

Amos stepped forward. "Not to be a buzzkill, but I don't think that's a good idea. There are some underlying issues to the problem at hand that need attention."

The elf huffed in annoyance. "Who's the one in charge here?"

Mistletoe started to raise her hand in the air, but I spoke before she could volunteer herself. I refused to allow the fairy to take the fall for any of the predicament. "Pandora Ashmore. A-S-H-M-O-R-E," I spelled out. "Although she seems to have scuppered off somewhere since nobody knows where she is."

Shrub, who had been standing stock still during the whole exchange, looked up at the Yeti who was watching him. The two shared a strange silent exchange, and alarm bells sounded in my head.

"She will need to answer for this debacle," the elf stated. "Who is in charge in the meantime?"

I nodded at the fairy, and Mistletoe floated forward with a little more confidence. "That would be me. I'll make sure everyone is informed and evacuate the premises as best as I can. In the meantime, I'll keep a small team working on the immediate issue to see if we can fix the source of the problem."

The elf agreed to the terms and stomped away from us, her phone already glued to her ear. The guard placed a hand on Shrub's shoulder. "I'll take this one away."

"No, I don't think that's a good idea," I interjected, pointing my finger at the two. "I think he should be taken to the station and held there."

"For what reason?" Topper asked in total confusion.

"Under suspicion of sabotage," Mistletoe stated in a clear voice. I guessed that stepping up as the boss again had bolstered her belief in herself.

Shrub sneered. "You can't prove anything. All you've got is her word that she heard me say something, not actual proof. And if that's good enough to land me in jail, then it's not like you're completely innocent in all this. Weren't you the one who said you wished you could figure out how to make all of this fail and expose Pandora as a fake?"

"Stop making things up to try and seem like you're innocent," I told the gremlin. "Mistletoe would never say something like that."

The tips of the fairy's wings quivered in response, but she kept her mouth shut. Amos and I caught

Topper up on what was going on with the rising temperature and the stones along the perimeter of the structure.

After hearing everything, the older man scratched his bald head. "Well, until you can figure things out, I guess I can take this here Scrub with me to the station."

The Yeti opened his mouth to say something but decided against it. Whatever connection those two had, the guard didn't want to give it away. I'd have to remind myself to ask Alfie about his colleague later. He stalked off to go back outside.

Topper took the gremlin with him as he instructed Mistletoe to start getting people to exit the bubble as quickly as possible. Nutty volunteered to go tell our friends Makai and Kailani about the situation. The fairy summoned a few employees that she trusted to help organize the necessary exodus of all the others.

I didn't know whether I should help get people out or go with Mistletoe and Amos to inspect more of the pots around the border. About the time I needed to decide what to do, I spotted Wyatt heading our way.

"Where have you been?" I called out to him, closing the distance between us.

He captured me in a quick hug. "After I tried to

help the workers at the bar look for Santa's snow, I realized I wasn't really doing anything to help. So, I decided to try and locate Pandora. Imagine my surprise when I found out nobody knew where she was or had even seen her since first thing this morning."

I took his hand and we joined Amos and Mistletoe. "There's so much you've missed, including how much more important it is that we find Pandora. More of the truth behind everything has been revealed."

My boyfriend lifted his eyebrow in suspicion. "Really? Would it have anything to do with how she supposedly isn't in charge of the event planning business and that all of this is actually Mistletoe's fault?"

My jaw dropped. "How did you know?"

Wyatt enjoyed my expression of shock with a smug grin. His spell phone pinged in his pocket, and he took it out to check his messages. "I guess you'll find out right now since she's being escorted inside as we speak."

He pointed at the main entrance, and I watched a woman dressed in nondescript winter attire looking over her shoulder as she took short steps inside the bubble. A hat with a puffy pom-pom on top covered up her hair, but as soon as she whipped it off, I recognized the color.

"Is that Pandora?" I squinted at the figure.

Wyatt chuckled. "Yep. Looks a lot different at the moment, but I think that was on purpose. Wait until you here where she was found."

The unhappy planner frowned over her shoulder at whoever was following behind her, but she didn't put up much of an argument. As soon as I recognized the large figure of the rock troll, I understood why.

"Rocky!" I shouted.

He offered me a two-fingered wave as he carried something covered by one of Wyatt's bar towels in his other hand. "Hey, Rory. I heard you might be looking for something you lost."

Pandora stumbled a bit as she struggled to navigate through the sand in her winter boots, almost as if not wearing her signature stilettos threw her off balance. She grumbled as she shed her heavy coat.

When she reached where our group, she glared at every single one of us. "What are you gawking at? I thought you were supposed to be getting people out, not forcing them to come back in."

"And I thought you were supposed to be the one in charge. And yet, when things go wrong, you just abandon the whole thing?" I accused. Without waiting for her answer, I shot a question at my friend. "Rocky, where did you find her?"

"I was watching Wyatt's bar for him, not that many people go there during the day. But he'd told me he was expecting a shipment to come in, so I took my portable reading device with me and read while I waited," the troll explained.

"I guess nobody told you that all shipments in or out of Holiday Haven had been canceled," I said.

Rocky shrugged one shoulder. "It didn't bother me none as I like the solitude to read. At some point, I went to the kitchen to grab a snack, and while I was there, I got Wyatt's message about Pandora going missing. He said that there was some sort of big reason why she needed to be found. I figured I'd go get Clarence's help since he'd spent more time with her, but as soon as I exited the kitchen, imagine my surprise when I found her inside the Break Room, clutching this."

The troll took off the towel to reveal the metal container with Santa's snow inside it.

"That's where it disappeared to," I declared, still a little confused. "But why would you take it?" I asked her.

She wouldn't even meet my gaze. Sweat trickled down the side of her face, and the planner wouldn't even get rid of her sweater to make herself more comfortable. Instead, she crossed her arms over her chest and screwed her lips into a tight bow.

"Judge me all you want, but I'm not answering any of your questions," she threatened. "And if you're looking for someone to blame, then you better turn your accusations against her." Pandora pointed a manicured finger at her former assistant.

"But I'm confused," I said, not allowing her to deflect the blame she so rightly deserved. "I thought you wanted all the credit for everything that happened. You can't hog all the glory if things go well and deny any responsibility if they don't."

Pandora's eyes found mine. "That's rich coming from you. You soaked up all the attention when everybody praised your name and worshipped your accomplishment like it was something big. All you did was create a sleigh, something that anybody could have provided if they'd looked in their garages. But then you go and cry when an article comes out that shows you aren't perfect after all."

"There's a big difference between reality and fiction," Rocky stated, his gravelly voice making her jump.

"Yeah, yeah." Nutty had rejoined us, and scampered to stand right in front of her, making her cringe away from him. "You probably made up everything and gave it to the Enquirer in the first place, didn't you?"

Pandora sniffed with resentment. "I'm pretty sure the article said unnamed source."

"But when you were talking to Shrub during the

blackout, he threatened to go to your source at the Enquirer. He said he would tell them about whatever it was you'd been asking him to do for you." With careful eyes, I watched for the planner's reaction.

Her mouth popped into a tiny *O* for a brief second. "I don't know who's been telling you lies—"

"Heard it with my own ears," I cut her off. "And I wasn't the only one. I wonder what it would take to get Shrub to give us more details now that he's been caught."

Her eyes darted about as if searching for a quick escape. "I'm not sure who this Shrub person is that you're talking about."

Amos huffed in disbelief. "You know, the gremlin who had been adding fire stones to your heating system?"

"There are several employees working behind the scenes. How am I meant to know what each one of them does?" Pandora held up her hands. "You know what, this is all hearsay. Unless you're psychic, I don't think you can prove anything. In fact, I don't think you have a shred of proof that I have any involvement in this disaster. So, I think I'll be leaving."

Mistletoe had been hiding behind our little crowd until that moment. Her pent-up anger over Pandora's betrayal came pouring out. The fairy blasted forward and waved her wand at her colleague.

"You won't be going anywhere." Much like the gremlin before, the fairy's magic lifted Pandora in the air, taking away her ability to escape.

"How dare you use your magic against me," Pandora seethed. "You have no right!"

"I have every right after what you did to me and especially for what you were trying to saddle me with by leaving," Mistletoe defended.

The planner stopped struggling against the fairy's power. "I don't know what you're talking about. Sounds to me like you're trying to ruin my reputation. I should sue you for that, but I'm sure I won't have to do that in order to ruin you. The fact that this whole scheme is going to collapse will be enough to do that."

"If you knew there was something wrong, then why didn't you do something to fix it?" I pushed in exasperation. "There are people at risk in here. And outside."

Pandora glared at me, pure hatred radiating out of her. "You don't get to ask me any questions. As far as I'm concerned, I don't have to answer to any of you."

A gust of wind blew around us, bringing relief with some much-needed cool air. The force of the gale strengthened and focused until it swirled in the middle of our group. Snowflakes and sparkles whirled into a concentrated vortex, and the strong scent of peppermint surrounded us. As soon as the winter maelstrom dissipated, Clara Claus stood in front of the floating planner.

"But you do have to answer to me," she commanded.

Chapter Thirteen

Before she confronted Pandora, Clara explained that she had brought a few people with her to help evacuate all the workers. She assured me that several of the North Pole coven were attempting to make an appropriate temporary lodging for those who were less suited for our area's weather.

Once safety measures were in place, at Clara's behest, Mistletoe released Pandora and set her gently down on the ground. Her former boss shot the fairy a nasty glance.

Santa's wife, and the head witch in charge, faced Pandora. "Well, now that I'm here, I'd like to hear your explanation of what's going on."

For the first time, the planner showed a modicum of humility. She jutted her lip out in a perfect pout.

"I'm so sorry for the trouble, Mrs. Claus, but these people are trying to persecute me when I had very little to do with any of this mess."

A loud snort escaped me, and I couldn't be bothered to cover up my reaction. Pandora switched from indignation to her "poor me" routine with expert ease while her accent thickened more than I thought possible.

"Is that so?" Clara closed her mouth, not adding anything else. Her neutral expression gave nothing away.

Pandora waited a tense moment before speaking again. "They are trying to pin the problems associated with this place and everything leading up to the event, on me. I'm sorry, but I don't see how any of it could be my fault."

Clara placed her hands behind her back. "Could you give me more details? What kinds of things are they blaming you for?"

In her excitement to get the rest of us in trouble, Pandora spoke in rapid succession. "First of all, I have done my absolute best to plan this amazing event for Holiday Haven. And from the very beginning, it has been an absolute nightmare to get my staff to do things the right way. I mean, I should be lauded for pulling off an entire beach inside this bubble. And I managed to bring in some amazing employees. Who else could have thought of mermaid lifeguards for the swimming area?"

"That sounds like fun," Clara admitted. "What else?"

Pandora pointed in the direction of the breaking waves. "I managed to have an entire ocean area conjured. All with a sandy beach and sea creatures. I brought a tropical environment right here to the North Pole."

"That sounds like an amazing feat to accomplish, especially getting all the permits approved for that magnitude of magic usage." A slight mischievous gleam shined in Mrs. Claus's eyes.

The planner bit her lip. "I mean, with a limited time to achieve it all, I maybe had to cut a few corners. But surely, that doesn't qualify me to be harassed and slandered."

"So, let me see if I'm understanding you," Clara's tone remained pleasant and friendly. "You were the one who put together the entire plan and executed it."

Caught up in the attention from Santa's wife, Pandora nodded with enthusiasm. "Exactly."

"And, if you don't mind me saying so, someone who could pull this off should be planning much bigger events. Maybe even working at the main workshop at the district center," Mrs. Claus continued.

I couldn't believe my ears. Was Clara buying into Pandora's story? Could she not see the manipulation that the rest of us could?

Pandora's eyes widened with greed. "Oh, Mrs. Claus, I would be so honored. It's all I've wanted ever since arriving here." She practically salivated, having her dreams handed to her on a silver platter.

Clara held up one finger. "Although, I don't quite understand something. Maybe you can clear it up for me. If everything is going so well, then what are the problems they are accusing you of neglecting?"

"That one," the planner pointed at me. "She has been a problem this whole time."

Santa's wife turned to face me for the first time. "Who, Aurora? But according to what I read, you were happy to have her involvement."

"Oh, yes, I was," Pandora stammered.

"And, let me see if I can get the quote right, that 'having an ice sculpture as a centerpiece would be a shining beacon to bring in as many residents as possible to the event.' Did I get your words right?" Clara asked.

"Uh, I suppose I might have said something like that." The planner's cheeks reddened. "However, she has been less than professional in how she's interacted. And the only work I've seen her produce was a sad snowman on the beach with just a straw hat and a pair of sunglasses that I think came from one of our souvenir shops." Pandora sneered. "Not exactly the quality I would expect from the famous sleigh maker. I mean, the ice was in the process of melting anyway. When I touched it, it had a slight sheen of water on the surface."

I straightened to attention. "Wait a minute. What were you doing checking out my test sculpture?"

Pandora realized her mistake in talking too much, and she rung her hands in front of her. "I mean, I am the person in charge. I needed to check on your progress. How was I to know that the pathetic thing was just a test?"

"You could have asked me," I replied. "But I think you had a different purpose in inspecting my snowman. You said you touched it to see how it was holding up. You wanted it to melt, didn't you?" As if hit by a strike of lightning, I saw the whole scenario with new clarity. "That explains your shift to have me do a sculpture at the end of your press conference. You wanted me involved because you wanted to see a sculpture of mine fail."

"That's...that's not...you're twisting my words," she said in a shaky voice.

Mistletoe floated to the front of our group. "Oh, Pandora. It was you."

"What?" the planner snapped. "I did nothing!"

"You knew the system put in place to heat the bubble was delicate. That each of the stones and crystals had to be in just the right configuration to channel the magic without a problem." The fairy shook her head in disappointment. "You raised the temperature to try and melt Rory's work."

Pandora took a step back, her body tensing as if in preparation to run. "Again, more speculation, more lies. You can't prove any of that, and I'm glad you're here, Mrs. Claus, to witness this...this...unwarranted attack."

"I am your witness," Clara agreed. "To you being willing to take the credit when things are going well. But what about when things started going wrong? What did you do then? How did you captain your ship and help your team?" Santa's wife matched the planner's step to get closer. "Did you stay here and help find solutions? Or did you run?"

"I...I..." Pandora's breath quickened until she exploded in a burst of words. "Listen, the magic involved wasn't mine to begin with. It was all Mistletoe's," she accused. "If anyone's to blame for the heating problem, talk to her."

Clara considered the latest allegation in silence. She pulled a phone out of her pocket and typed something into it. When she finished, she turned to face the fairy. "Is it true?"

Mistletoe held her head up high. "I am responsible for how the whole system was set up and the initial magic flowing through it. It is also my power that created everything inside and the bubble containing it all. So, maybe when Pandora says it's my fault, it really is."

"There," the planner snapped. "She admits her guilt."

"No, she explained what she should be credited for," Clara said.

"But it was all my idea," Pandora pouted.

Mrs. Claus's patience ran thin. "You are trying to ride both sides of the fence right now. Either you are responsible for it all or she is. But what I find more concerning is your choice not to care enough about the people working for you. You should have stayed and tried to figure out a solution."

"But I was," the planner whined. "I took some of that secret ingredient that the bartenders were using in their drinks. I wanted to see if I could figure out its magical properties and use it to create a charm to fix the situation."

Rocky held up the small metal container. "Did you seriously believe that this tiny amount in here could cool this entire space?" The troll gestured at the dome above us.

Clara shook her head. "Once again, affecting someone else's magic to try and create your own outcome. And while your intent may have held the slightest hint of help, you would not have been able to unravel the charm to make it your own."

Pandora sniffed with contempt. "Why not?"

"Because that snow was made with my magic," Mrs. Claus declared.

I sneaked a peek at Wyatt and mouthed 'I knew it!' at him.

"Ah, here is someone who I believe can be of help to us in this moment. Officer, thank you so much for backtracking and returning for me." Clara waved Topper and his charge over.

Shrub practically vibrated with anger. "First you wanted me gone and now you brought me back. I wish I'd never taken this job."

"Who hired you?" Clara asked.

The gremlin pointed a crooked finger at Pandora. "She pays so she's the boss."

"And what did she pay you to do?" Santa's wife pressed.

Pandora licked her lips in nervous agitation.

Shrub placed his hands in the pockets of his overalls. "If she needed something done, I was the one to do it."

Clara didn't care for his dismissive attitude. She bent down until she confronted him at his eye level. "Details, my friend, are important. What exactly were some of the things she needed done?"

The gremlin's leathery ears shivered with sudden nerves. "She wanted me to find a way to increase the heat inside. Said she wouldn't allow this Rory person to hog all the glory."

"He lies," Pandora squeaked. "He's the one who sabotaged things. After all, he's a gremlin and that's what they do, right?"

Her attack on the small creature broke whatever agreement he had with her. Shrub spit on the ground in the planner's direction. "She also wanted things to fail on some level. That way she could place the blame on the fairy and lay claim to the whole business. Oh, and it was her idea to bury more of the hot stones to increase the heat no matter the cost. And when things were getting worse today, she had me pay one of the guards out front to make sure she got away without being seen."

Clara nodded at Topper, who escorted the tiny gremlin away again. "I think I've heard everything I need to make a decision."

"Wait a minute, I didn't know I was on trial," Pandora complained. "Shouldn't I be offered a lawyer or something?"

"Oh, official justice will come later for you," Santa's wife promised. "But right now, you need to make amends for your choices."

Pandora crossed her arms. "I'm not apologizing to any of them."

"I'm not talking about an apology, although more than one is owed," Clara said.

A large crash followed by rumbling thunder vibrated our bodies. For the first time, I paid attention to the unusual sky above us.

Inside the dome, a bright light acted as the sun, bathing us in intense heat. But outside, dark clouds made it look like nighttime had fallen early. Another deafening boom of thunder shook the ground underneath us.

Clara pointed at the way out. "Your first act of restitution will be to help with what's brewing outside. Come on, everybody. Let's go save the North Pole."

Chapter Fourteen

Instead of waiting for us to put our winter clothes back on, Clara flicked her fingers in the air. In a whoosh of orange and cloves, our outfits morphed into matching winter attire.

Wyatt zipped up my white puffy coat and flipped the hood over my head with a little too much mirth. "Now who's the snowman?"

I stuck my tongue out at him. "Let's head outside before this snowman melts from the heat in here."

Following Mrs. Claus, we slogged through the sand in our winter boots to get to the exit. The second she pulled the flap wide for us to walk through, a heavy blast of air almost blew me backwards. Wyatt caught me and kept his hands wrapped around my arms to help me move forward.

The muddy ground should have stained our

outfits, but whatever charm created them, it kept us pristine. The circumference of land no longer covered by snow expanded all the way into the woods.

"That happened since we were inside?" I marveled.

Clara stepped up beside me, holding onto Pandora. "That's why I brought a little back up with me."

Several people were gathered around the beach bubble. Vale and her mom stood at the front. Aster nodded once to Mrs. Claus, who dipped her head in some form of a signal. Vale's mother talked to the other witches around her, pointing and signaling. In a few moments, those who could help spread out until they formed a circle. I could just make out the faintest noise of chanting while they outstretched their arms and turned their faces skyward.

I pushed back a strand of hair that had whipped in front of my face and dared to look up, too. An ominous cloud, dark as night, swirled over the top of the dome.

Pandora struggled to get away. "Let me go."

"If that's what you want, then by all means, leave." Clara released her.

The planner bolted a few steps away and stopped, turning around to face Mrs. Claus. "It can't be as easy as that."

"It's a choice," Clara stated. "You can stay here and help fix what you caused or you can go save yourself. I am not going to force you to do anything. It's all about what you can live with."

Pandora grabbed the edges of her hood to keep the wind from blowing it off her head. She stomped off in the direction of the woods.

"You're going to let her go?" I shouted at Santa's wife.

"This part has to be on her. Plus, I have faith." She tipped her head in the direction of Pandora's escape.

The planner scooted through the circle of the coven members but only made it a couple of feet away. She slowed down and glanced over her shoulder at the sky above us. Stomping her foot once, she turned around and forced her way into the circle next to Aster, adding her magic despite the deep glower on her face.

Amos slapped me on the back and joined the other witches. Rocky bent down to allow Nutty to scramble into his cradled hands. The two other Humbugs went to join the spectators who were safe behind the circle.

Mistletoe's wand glowed bright, her magic keeping her steady in the heavy winds. Clara beckoned the fairy to join us.

Knowing I had a part to play, I looked to Wyatt

for reassurance, and he kissed my cheek. "You've got this."

I soaked in the confidence of his words to battle my own doubts. Sending my boyfriend away with a quick peck on the lips, I took in a deep breath to steady myself.

A bright flash of lightning lit up the darkened sky, and thunder cracked and rumbled. The force of the wind picked up, and rain mixed with sleet whipped around us.

"We don't have any time to lose," Clara explained. "The coven members are here to back us up, but I'm going to need both of you to stay in the center of it all," she shouted over the unnatural tumult. "Mistletoe, since this originates with your magic, despite all of Pandora's interference, we'll need you to keep things as steady as possible until I give you the signal. And then, I'll need you to undo everything as fast as you can. Can you do that?"

For someone so small, the fairy possessed a lot of bravery. She brandished her wand in front of her much like the knights of old preparing to battle a dragon. "I can do it."

Clara bobbed her head with approval. "And then there's you." She turned to me, her demeanor remaining regal and assured.

I clenched my hands into fists. "What do you need me to do?"

The head witch smiled wide. "Once again, I'm going to need your special magic, my friend. This storm is brewing because of the clash between the magical heat leaking from the bubble and the cold air of the region. Think of it as two giants fighting to see who gets control. And who gets hurt when giants fight?"

"All those in their way," I answered. "But I'm not sure I can create anything out of ice that will do any good."

She shook her head. "You're not making anything this time. When I tell you to, I want you to blast both your fire and ice magic at the center of that swirl." Clara pointed at the monster of a storm. "If you can, keep your streams separate so you can adjust with heat or ice as needed to affect the temperature. Don't worry, I'll be right beside you to assist."

I stared at her, fear squeezing my heart. "How do you know I can do this?"

Clara placed her hand on my arm. "You've earned more than my faith with your path in life." She squeezed me once. "Besides, after the whole sleigh thing, this'll be a piece of cake. You had to do that all on your own."

I glanced around us at everyone helping, even Pandora. Wyatt stood right behind Vale, and he winked at me. My insides warmed, and I felt ready to take on the challenge. "It takes a team," I said, getting her meaning.

"Exactly."

An elf ran out of the dome and reported to Clara. Whatever he said, it pleased Santa's wife. She gave him a few instructions and sent him on his way. "Okay, everyone who was inside is out and safe. It's time."

Raising her hand in the air, she signaled to Aster, and the chanting grew a little louder.

"I've got this. I've got this," Mistletoe repeated to herself.

The fairy concentrated with all her might, and the tip of her wand gleamed so bright I had to squint to watch. her. She gritted her teeth, and a pale pink barrier extended in front of her. At first, it approached the edge of the beach bubble with slow progress, but as soon as it touched the outer limit, the fairy's new magic overtook her old efforts. In a matter of seconds, a pale pink shimmer coated the whole bubble like a magical liquid.

Mistletoe's control of things took immediate effect. The swirling storm above slowed down a fraction.

Clara touched my shoulder. Before she could say anything, I lifted my chin. "It's my turn," I said.

Sticking my tongue out, I summoned my powers and channeled them in a way I never had before.

Months ago, when I'd first arrived in Holiday Haven, I wouldn't have trusted my own magic for such a difficult task. But now, I knew I hadn't even begun to reach my limits. With my magical energies coursing through me, I held up both hands.

"Try to cool things down first," Clara suggested.

Widening my fingers on my left hand, I willed my magic through my palm. Magic so cold that it stung burst out of me, and my whole body recoiled a little from the force of the blast. I widened my feet into a stronger stance and stood my ground.

The icy blue stream of power hit the cloud, and after a few seconds, the color of the clouds lightened from pitch black to a hazy gray. The rain pelting us turned into a light icy mix.

"I can't believe it's working," I exclaimed with a nervous laugh.

My words came out too soon as the cloud color changed again. The swirling vortex at the center of the weather mass sped up.

Clara watched with great concern. "It's fighting to find balance. Try adding some heat."

I flexed my fingers on my right hand. Furrowing my brow in concentration, I sent a hot red stream of concentrated fire magic directly to the center of the massive cloud. Like a living monster, the vortex in the middle widened, and the stream disappeared into the gaping maw of the whirlwind. Instead of improving the situation, I'd made the storm above worse.

Gale force winds rushed around us, and I fought hard not to stumble. My stream of fire energy faltered, and Mistletoe tumbled in the air, her wand blown away from her. The pale pink shimmer encasing the bubble faded in and out.

I dove after the wand and snatched it before it blew away. Clara held the fairy by her waist, keeping her steady. I handed Mistletoe her wand, and once she got her bearings again, she flicked the wand, keeping the containment field alive.

"You got any other suggestions?" I shouted over the windy tumult at Clara.

"Do what you think is best," she said, still holding onto the fairy.

If the individual sides of my magic weren't enough to help, then maybe I needed to stop trying to keep them separate. After all, it took both my fire and ice powers working together to create my sculptures. Maybe it would take a mixture of them in order to kill the storm.

Placing the heels of my hands together, I let both of my energies stream out of my hands. Instead of keeping them separate, I mixed the two flows together, unsure of what would happen. I took aim at the center of the chaos in the sky and blasted it with everything I had.

"I don't know how much longer I can hold on," Mistletoe cried out.

Willing more energy to flow through me, I pushed more of my mix at the storm, crying out at the effort. About the time I was ready to give up, the shadowy clouds lightened again, and the small pellets of ice pelting against us softened to a billowy snow. The wind died down enough so that Mistletoe could fly on her own.

Clara took a step away from the fairy. "Here's our window. You have to get rid of the whole thing, Mistletoe."

"I'll try," the fairy gritted.

I kept feeding the streams aimed at the slowing clouds to give her as much time as I could. With a little shriek of effort, Mistletoe brandished her wand in the air. Twirling it above her three times, she aimed a blast from the end of it right at the structure.

A bright flash of light rebounded off the dome, and I ducked my head, fighting to keep my magic flowing. I watched the beach bubble shiver and shake until it shrank a few feet. Mistletoe flew toward it, and the closer she got, the whole structure diminished little by little.

Clara touched my shoulder to get my attention. "That's enough, Rory. You did good."

With intent, I stopped the energy flow and fell forward, gripping my knees to hold me up.

Distracted by watching the fairy, I hadn't noticed my own reserves depleting. Strong arms wrapped around me, and I leaned into Wyatt as he held me up.

Mistletoe's tiny body shook, pale pink dust floating down from her shivering wings as she hovered above a tiny sparkling ball. At that size, the beach bubble resembled a snow globe. With one final wave of her wand, Mistletoe finished off the last of the dome. Exhausted, she drifted out of the air until her feet touched the ground. Her wings quivered with fatigue, and the coven rushed to her aid.

"And now," Clara said with a relieved smile, "it's my turn."

Santa's wife raised both hands in the air. The blast of magic that emanated from her pushed us back a few steps. The scent of pine, mulled spices, roasted chestnuts, a crackling fire, and other holiday smells surrounded us. Cold air rushed around, replacing the last of the summer heat. Glittering snowflakes danced in the wind, and when Clara finished her final charms, the whole sky burst into a steady snow.

"Now it's truly Christmas in July," Wyatt declared, opening his mouth to catch a flake on his tongue.

I laughed at his playfulness. "Based on what happened here today, I think you mean Witchmas in July!"

Chapter Fifteen

Istrummed the strings of my new ukulele, cringing when I hit a wrong note. Pulling the bridge of the instrument closer, I concentrated on where I'd placed my fingertips.

"Put your index finger here, your third finger here, and stretch your fourth finger to this string," Makai instructed me as I sat on the rock with the waves crashing around us. "There. Now strum up and down like I taught you."

I strummed a couple of times until the chord came out clearer than before. "I think it's going to take more than one lesson for me to play a full song," I joked, still trying to get my finger to move up and down in rhythm.

"After this celebration event, you can come visit me and Kailani anytime. I think you'd love the waters off Oahu." Makai leaned back into the conjured sea and splashed me with his tail.

Kailani swam next to Hina and joined us. "Is my brother bothering you about visiting again?" She rolled her eyes at him, and he splashed her as well. "Although, since I heard all about your incredible magic, maybe you should come and visit. I'll teach you all about Pele, our own Goddess of fire and volcanoes."

I held onto my small ukulele. "I'd say my ice powers wouldn't work there, but ever since I was able to create the new sculpture, I'm pretty sure I can figure out a way to make things work there, too."

Makai swam a little closer. "I wish we could see your carvings. It's all anyone is talking about."

I didn't think about the fact that the mermaids wouldn't have a way to visit where I'd fashioned my piece. Pulling out my spell phone, I chose the best picture out of the bunch. "Here. I'll take a better one next time I pass by it."

The brother and sister floated forward, staring at the image. "Is that..." Kailani pointed at herself.

Makai hugged an emerging Koa about his broad shell. "Braddah, you a superstar now," the burly mermaid exclaimed. "And you managed to capture my best side."

"Your left?" I asked.

He winked at me. "Nah. All sides are my best

side," Makai bragged. He glanced over his shoulder at the swimmers teetering on the edge of the swimming platform. "Gotta go, duty calls. Hey, Rory. Thanks, sistah."

Kailani wiped a tear from her cheek and hugged Hina close. "It's very beautiful. I'm honored."

I swallowed hard, overcome by my emotions. "The honor is mine. I'll definitely check my schedule and see if Wyatt and I can coordinate a time to visit with you. I could definitely use more inspiration for my work."

Kailani blew me a kiss and swam off to help her brother.

Taking the ukulele with me, I got up and walked through the warm sand to the lounge chairs. A sprite dressed in an employee uniform approached me as soon as I sat down.

"What can I get you?" she asked, her ponytail bobbing back and forth.

I almost asked for a Fire and Ice, but decided I'd get something a little less self-centered. "How about one of Santa's Slushies?"

"Cool. Be right back." The sprite dashed off, and I swung my legs onto the lounger and leaned back to enjoy the pleasant warmth coming from the sunlight above.

I let out a long sigh and closed my eyes. "If this is a dream, may I never wake up."

A shadow fell over me, and I peeked through one eye to figure out who dared to block the light.

"Is the seat next to you taken?" a familiar voice asked.

I sat up to face Clara. "Considering you helped create the new beach bubble, I'm pretty sure you can use any seat you want," I joked.

"I didn't do it all by myself. Mistletoe explained the whole layout, so it's still based off her work. I just tweaked the light source so we wouldn't create another potential disaster." Mrs. Claus pointed at the large crystal at the center of the dome. "I figured it was better to use the design to reflect the illumination from the actual sun. Combined with a warming charm, we get a much stabler atmosphere inside."

The sprite returned with my drink, and I offered it to Clara. The powerful witch declined and asked for a lemonade instead. "Don't tell my husband, but I've already had two of those."

I nibbled on the watermelon slice used as a garnish. "It was really nice of you to set one of these up in all of the towns and not just in Holiday Haven."

Clara knit her eyebrows. "I think Mistletoe's idea was a good one. Why shouldn't everybody in the North Pole celebrate the solstice with a little special brand of summer fun? After talking with everyone involved and sifting through all the details, it occurred to me that maybe the results of the Seasonal Spirit Awards had bred too much competition rather than an overall sense of community. My husband and I want to inspire cooperation, not encourage resentments."

I took too many sips of the drink and smacked my forehead. "Ooh, brain freeze." Sucking in air to help the sensation cease, I waited until the temporary pain passed. "I wish the press wouldn't make such a big deal out of me. I feel like all of the attention somehow created the problem with Pandora."

Clara took the lemonade from the sprite and thanked her, handing her a very large tip. "Pandora's actions are her own, and I think her banishment from the North Pole is a fitting beginning to her punishment for her choices.

"And trust me, you'll need to learn to handle attention. I have a feeling you'll be accomplishing many more things in your future that will garner praise and some scrutiny. You'll have to toughen up to weather things when the bad stuff comes your way if you're going to move on to bigger and better things." The ice cubes in her glass clinked as she took a drink, but I didn't miss the mischievous expression under her straw hat.

"You look like a cat with a secret. Way too smug for its own good," I accused. "Do you have some scheme involving me you'd like to share?"

She smacked her lips in satisfaction after swallowing a few gulps. "When you're ready, I'll let you know."

I opened my mouth to interrogate her further, but Nutty bounded across the sand and settled on my lap. "Amos sent me to find you. Told me to tell you that you should come over to the volleyball court."

"But I said I wanted to spend the day relaxing, not doing anything physical." Using my magic to help only two days earlier still had me drained.

"Oh, it's not to get you to play. He thought you should come see who he's playing against." Nutty scurried off me and stopped, turning around and scampering to sit on top of Clara's stomach. "Yeah, yeah, you too, Mrs. Claus."

It was impossible to resist my roommate's cuteness, so we followed his twitching tail all the way over to the volleyball courts. Wyatt tossed the ball up and down in the air, taunting the other team.

"If we're going to play, then let's make it interesting," he challenged.

My mouth gaped open at his opponent. Santa Claus stroked his beard while his belly jiggled as he chuckled. "You really want to bet against me?"

My boyfriend caught ball and spun it on the end of his finger before passing it off to one of his teammates. "You scared, old man?"

I sucked in a short breath. "Should he be talking like that to your husband?"

"Oh, he actually likes it," Clara said. "It does him good when he's treated like everybody else rather than a big celebrity."

Wyatt caught me admiring his naked torso, and he wiggled his eyebrows at me. With a little too much bravado, he flexed his muscles to show off his chiseled abs and bulging biceps.

"Oh, girl. You've got it bad," Clara teased me. "But you're not alone. Hubba hubba." She placed two fingers to her lips and wolf-whistled at Santa.

Her husband let out a jolly guffaw and mimicked Wyatt's poses. His old-fashioned striped bathing outfit hugged every single curve on him.

Amos sat in the official's chair ready to call the game. "Quit horsing around and get to playing."

Santa pulled his sunglasses down his nose and approached the net. "Okay, what are the stakes?"

Wyatt stroked his chin. "If my team wins, then we each get to take a joyride in your sleigh." He glanced over at me. "And we each get to bring one person with us."

I scrunched up my nose. "I've still got an offer to ride in the sleigh and bring Wyatt with me that I've never cashed in on."

"Yeah, but your man just secured the deal for the

rest of his team. Which is a pretty generous gesture," Clara said.

"And if my team wins and sends your team Ho-Ho-Home, then we each get three months' worth of the good stuff." Santa pushed his glasses up his nose and extended his hand.

His wife groaned. "Of course he would negotiate a deal for moonshine. I'll never be able to tame that boy."

I bumped her shoulder with mine. "Would you really want to?"

She giggled. "Absolutely not."

"Deal!" Wyatt agreed, shaking hands under the net.

"Excellent," Amos grunted. "Based on the coin toss that happened like a million years ago, Wyatt's team serves first."

Wanting to show my loyalty, I raised my hands to either side of my mouth and shouted, "Come on, honey. You can do it!"

"You think your man can beat mine?" Clara asked.

The corner of my lip quirked up. "I'd wager on it."

"Terms?"

I knew exactly what I wanted. "A lifetime supply of the best coffee in the world."

Clara raised her eyebrow. "That's all?"

"My needs are simple." Of course, I could have asked for something much more valuable, but a bet between friends should always include fun stakes. "And you?"

"If the big guy's team wins, then I want you to come to the castle once a week and consider training under me." She clapped her hands as Wyatt served the first ball.

I stared at her, missing the beginning of the game. "Why would you want that?"

"Good hit, honey," she called out to her husband. After applauding, she turned to face me. "For one, I enjoy your company. Two, we have very similar magic, and I would like to take you on to teach you a few things."

Now, I couldn't decide whether I wanted to see Wyatt win or lose. I opened my mouth to ask another question, but Clara interrupted me.

"And three, my husband and I are getting up there in age. At some point and time, we'll have to step down. You never know who might be best to take over. Might as well get a jump start on trying to find a potential candidate." She took my hand in hers. "Deal?"

I shook on it without even realizing I had solidified a very interesting bet. With so much at stake, I stepped closer to the game, watching every point as if the journey my life might take depended on it.

Epilogue

I placed each bag of enticing coffee beans in the cupboard next to my new coffee mug that declared Home is where the heart is, except instead of the word heart, there was a silhouette of a bear with a heart emoji over its fur.

Wyatt handed me another bag. "When Clara pays up on her bet, she doesn't mess around."

"I know." I'd have to make room on a different shelf or find another place to store the rest still left in the box. "She said since I didn't know exactly which coffee was the absolute best, I should try a little of everything. I didn't think she'd send me something from everywhere in the world."

"Even though you won the bet, are you still going to meet with her every week? I think it's a huge opportunity," Wyatt said.

I squeezed the cup to my chest. "I know, but I've never really had anybody teach me how to use my magic properly. And she's right, she does have the closest powers to me. Her knowledge would be invaluable."

Wyatt tried his best to seem casual while he asked the next question. "And the other part you told me about?"

"What, the whole thing about her and Santa retiring and needing a replacement?" I scoffed. "I think she was just trying to make her bet look good. There's no way it's a real offer."

"And what if it was?" he pressed. "Have you given any thought to that possibility?"

When I allowed my brain time to think about it, I had obsessed about the whole thing. But knowing Clara, nothing was a done deal, and she would only offer me choices and never force me into anything.

I blew out a long sigh. "Nope. Not gonna go down that road tonight."

In an attempt to distract me, Wyatt read the back of the next package. "You know, I've heard there's a treasured coffee bean that gets consumed by an animal, and then the beans are collected and roasted after it...you know..."

It took me a moment to get his meaning. "Eww, please tell me I don't have any of that." Racing over to snatch the bag out of his hand, I searched the label.

He chuckled at my response. "Guess you're going to have to figure it out on your own." Wyatt stopped inspecting the contents of the box and leaned against the counter. "You sure you're good with your decision? You don't think you were pushed into making it too quickly?"

I unwrapped a plate while I pondered his questions. "No, I think it was definitely time for me to make a move." Placing the plate on the counter, I closed the distance between us and threw my arms around his muscular shoulders. "Have I thanked you lately?"

"Um, I don't think I can remember if you have. Why don't you remind me?" he teased.

Standing on my tiptoes, I met his mouth with mine and sunk into him. A satisfied growl rumbled in his chest, and I nipped on his lips, pleased that my kisses caused noises like that from my man.

A knock on the front door interrupted us, and I pulled away with reluctance. "I guess I should try to get to know the neighbors," I sighed.

I pranced over to answer the second round of knocks with giddy anticipation. The second I pulled the door open, my heart warmed at my visitor. "Hey, Nutty."

"Howdy, neighbor." The squirrel scampered

inside. "I wanted to officially welcome you to the neighborhood by giving you a box of my best nuts, but someone ate them before I got here."

I placed a hand on my hip. "You managed to eat all of them in the fifty paces from your door to my door?"

When I'd had the time to consider Wyatt's original offer to have me move in with him, I knew I wasn't ready to take that big of a leap. However, with my business thriving, it really made sense for me to move out and try living on my own. To make it an easier transition on me, and especially my squirrel buddy, I made an offer on the next-door cabin so that we'd both still have each other nearby.

Nutty licked his little paws and cleaned his mouth. "I guess I'll have to get you a different housewarming gift. But I can't stay long." He rushed over to me and hugged my ankle. "Just wanted to say hi. And to tell you to come over whenever you want."

"You, too," I offered without thinking about it. "As long as you knock first before entering," I added for good measure, calling out to my former roommate as he made his way to the door.

"Yeah, yeah," Nutty agreed. A cold wind blew a few flakes of snow inside as he left.

I closed the door, already missing my little buddy. I'd no longer wake up to him jumping up and down on my chest. Or squeezing my face between his tiny paws. Or crawling under the blankets with me for some extra minutes of shared warmth.

I dashed a stray tear away and tried to hide it from Wyatt, but the big bear caught me up in his arms and hugged me. "Big changes sometimes come with a little heartache. It's okay to feel sad."

Giving into my feelings, I cried into his chest for what I was losing for a few moments. After I let it all out, I sniffed and focused on the promise of what might come.

Wyatt let go of me and dug around in one of my boxes, unwrapping dishes until he found two bowls and set them on the counter. "I thought you might need a little cheering up, so I think I'm going to give you my housewarming present now."

He pulled out a plastic container and took out two large cookies and placed them in the bowls. "These are my Granny's shortcakes. Made them from a recipe passed down in our family. In truth, she used to say put in a little bit of this and a handful of that. But eventually, we convinced her to give us actual measurements to use." He retrieved another container full of fresh-cut strawberries.

"Let me guess, you used your Santa connection again?" I asked.

"Mm-hmm," he said as he poured strawberries on top of the shortcakes. He glanced back at me with a raised eyebrow, and with a sweet smile, he shook out a few more berries into the bowl on the right. "Now, I brought some fresh whipped cream as an option, but in my family, we like to pour some cold milk over it and enjoy the sweetness of the fruit. Your choice."

I couldn't help but adore this man who had come up with the perfect gift. "I'll go with the milk."

"Good choice!" Wyatt pulled open the fridge and got the bottle of milk, splashing some into both bowls. "You'll make a good Berenger yet."

"Hey, I've just taken a giant step forward in my life, mister. Don't go pushing me from behind," I scolded, accepting the bowl with extra strawberries from him.

"Don't mind me. Just hopin' and dreamin' a little," he drawled in his alluring accent. He held up his bowl in the air. "Here's to your new home and possibilities. May they bring you joy and happiness."

I clinked my bowl against his and scooped some of the shortcake and fruit onto my spoon. The berries tasted sweet but didn't come close to how delicious it felt to have my own space to live my life however I wanted to. "I don't think I could be any happier than I am in this moment right now."

"Oh, challenge accepted, sweetheart," Wyatt growled.

We settled down on my new couch in front of the roaring fireplace. For now, I would savor the sweetness of summer and being with my boyfriend in my new home. With the solstice over, everything would switch into high gear while everybody in the North Pole prepared for the next Christmas. For the first time in my life, I couldn't wait to see what this year's holiday season would bring.

A Note from Bella -

Thank you so much for reading *Cheery Charms,* and please consider submitting a review! To keep reading more about Rory and the Humbugs, *Merry Mischief* is up next!

I hope you will enjoy the other Winter Witches of Holiday Haven stories as well:

Peppermint Pixies by Danielle Garrett
Jolly Jinxes by J. L. Collins
Holiday Hijinks by Elle Adams
Solstice Spirits by Erin Johnson

Join us in our Facebook reader group - The Coffee Cauldron

RECIPES

The Rory (Fire & Ice Cocktail)

- 8 oz Silver tequila
- 4 oz Lime tequila
- 12 Fresh strawberries

- 4 oz Fresh lime juice
- 2 oz Jalapeño Simple syrup
- 3 Tbs Tajin seasoning
- 2 scoops of Santa's Snow*

Santa's Snow availability may be limited to the magical community of Holiday Haven. If you cannot get your hands on some, you can substitute 2 cups of ice.

Combine all ingredients in a blender and mix until it reaches desired consistency. Adjust tartness by adding or reducing lime juice. More jalapeño simple syrup can be added to increase the spiciness. Moisten the rims of the glasses with a lime wedge and dip in tajin seasoning. Pour drink into the glass and garnish with a sliced strawberry.

Jalapeño Simple Syrup

- 1 cup water
- 2 cups Turbinado or Demerara sugar (regular brown sugar can be used but will increase the sweetness of the syrup)
- 2 Jalapeño peppers, rinsed and sliced

Bring the water to a boil over medium-high heat and add sugar, stirring until it dissolves. Once sugar is dissolved, add the slices of jalapeño, reducing the heat and simmering for 3-5 minutes while continuing to stir. Remove the pot from the heat and let it sit for 20-30 minutes. Strain to remove jalapeño slices and store in a sealed container. Keep refrigerated.

Santa's Slushy

- 4 cups cubed seedless watermelon
- 8 oz. vodka
- 4 oz. fresh lime juice
- 4 oz. simple syrup

- 1 scoop of Santa's Snow*

Blend all ingredients together. Serve with watermelon slices for garnish.

Santa's Snow availability may be limited to the magical community of Holiday Haven. If you cannot get your hands on some, you can blend all of the ingredients and pour into a container. Freeze for at least 4 hours and then let it thaw for 15 mins and scoop into glasses.

Granny's Strawberry Shortcake

- 1 1/2 cup Flour
- 1/2 to 2/3 cup Sugar
- 2 teaspoons Baking Powder
- 1/2 to 1 teaspoon Salt
- 1 Egg
- 1 stick of butter, slightly softened
- Milk

Preheat oven to 400 degrees. In glass bowl, sift together all dry ingredients. Add egg and butter, then use hands to mix ingredients. Add enough milk to make a soft dough but not a runny batter. Using a spoon, place dough onto a baking sheet. Recipe should make 4-6 scoops. Bake for about 10 minutes until they are golden brown on top and toothpick comes out of the domed middle clean.

Once cooled, place shortcake in a bowl. Add sliced (and sweetened if desired) strawberries on top. Top with milk or fresh whipped cream and enjoy!

Read all of the new
Winter Witches of Holiday Haven

BELLA FALLS

DANIELLE GARRETT

J. L. COLLINS

ELLE ADAMS

ERIN JOHNSON

Read all of the Winter Witches

Read the entire Winter Witches of Holiday Haven Series!

Sleigh Spells by Bella Falls
Reindeer Runes by Danielle Garrett
Holiday Hexes by J. L. Collins
Winter Wishes by Elle Adams
Cocoa Curses by Erin Johnson
Cheery Charms by Bella Falls
Peppermint Pixies by Danielle Garrett
Jolly Jinxes by J. L. Collins
Holiday Hijinks by Elle Adams
Solstice Spirits by Erin Johnson
Merry Mischief by Bella Falls
Evergreen Elves by Danielle Garrett
Icy Illusions by J. L. Collins

Tinsel Trickery by Elle Adams
Mistletoe Mojo by Erin Johnson

All of the stories take place in the same wonderful winterland of Holiday Haven! They can be read and enjoyed in any order!

Join the Coffee Cauldron reader group to get behind-the-scenes info, have a little holiday fun, and of course, join in some fun giveaways! Make it Witchmas all year long!

Also by Bella Falls

Southern Relics Cozy Mysteries

Flea Market Magic

Rags To Witches

Pickup and Pirates

Vintage Vampire

Bargain Haunting

A Southern Charms Cozy Mystery Series

Moonshine & Magic: Book 1

Lemonade & Love Potions: A Cozy Short

Fried Chicken & Fangs: Book 2

Sweet Tea & Spells: Book 3

Barbecue & Brooms: Book 4

Collards & Cauldrons: Book 5

Red Velvet & Reindeer: A Cozy Short

Cornbread & Crossroads: Book 6

Preserves & Premonitions: Book 7

Grits & Ghosts: Book 8 (Coming Soon)

*All audiobooks available are narrated by the wonderful and talented Johanna Parker

For a FREE exclusive copy of the prequel to the Southern

Charms series, Chess Pie & Choices, sign up for my newsletter!

Share recipes, talk about Southern Charms and all things cozy mysteries, and connect with me by joining my reader group Southern Charms Cozy Companions!

Hextra Free Stories

Want to read more about your favorite characters? Check out the free "hextra" stories available to all subscribers to my newsletter or members of my reader group Southern Charms Cozy Companions!

Click here to subscribe:

https://books.bookfunnel.com/bellasubscriberhextras

Click here to join:

Southern Charms Cozy Companions

Acknowledgments

I want to thank my fellow Winter Witches authors—Danielle Garrett, J.L. Collins, Elle Adams, and Erin Johnson. This has been a fun world to create with all of you!

About the Author

Bella Falls grew up on the magic of sweet tea, barbecue, and hot and humid Southern days. She met her husband at college over an argument of how to properly pronounce the word *pecan* (for the record, it should be *pea-cawn,* and they taste amazing in a pie). Although she's had the privilege of living all over the States and the world, her heart still beats to the rhythm of the cicadas on a hot summer's evening.

Now, she's taken her love of the South and woven it into a world where magic and mystery aren't the only Charms.

bellafallsbooks.com
contact@bellafallsbooks.com
Bella Falls' Newsletter
Southern Charms Cozy Companions

facebook.com/bellafallsbooks

twitter.com/bellafallsbooks

instagram.com/bellafallsbooks

amazon.com/author/bellafalls

bookbub.com/authors/bella-falls